GREAT IDEAS THAT WILL KEEP YOU STRESS-FREE & RELAXED AT WORK

Dr. Pratik P. Surana

Publishers
Pustak Mahal®, Delhi

J-3/16 , Daryaganj, New Delhi-110002
☎ 23276539, 23272783, 23272784 • *Fax:* 011-23260518
E-mail: info@pustakmahal.com • *Website:* www.pustakmahal.com

Sales Centre
- 10-B, Netaji Subhash Marg, Daryaganj, New Delhi-110002
  ☎ 23268292, 23268293, 23279900 • *Fax:* 011-23280567
  E-mail: rapidexdelhi@indiatimes.com
- 6686, Khari Baoli, Delhi-110006
  ☎ 23944314, 23911979

Branches
Bengaluru: ☎ 080-22234025 • *Telefax:* 080-22240209
E-mail: pustak@airtelmail.in • pustak@sancharnet.in

Mumbai: ☎ 022-22010941, 022-22053387
E-mail: rapidex@bom5.vsnl.net.in

Patna: ☎ 0612-3294193 • *Telefax:* 0612-2302719
E-mail: rapidexptn@rediffmail.com

Hyderabad: *Telefax:* 040-24737290
E-mail: pustakmahalhyd@yahoo.co.in

ISBN 978-81-223-1358-1

Edition 2012

Printed at : Param Offsetters, Delhi

Dedication

With profound gratitude I dedicate this book to:

The loving and very fond memories of my uncle whom I lost a year back, Late Shri Nandkishoreji Soni (my very own Nandu Uncle), who has always been there for me and made it specially to my first book launch despite of his hectic schedule.

I also dedicate it to my children, Krisha and Meghav, my entire family, wife Anshima, Mom, Dad, my sister Pragati, Bai and Babuji, and many friends… And to some very special persons in my life, Megha, Mehek, Sheri, Mano, Helen and many other very dear friends.

Acknowledgements

I must acknowledge the influence of various great people who have guided me through their books, articles and other writings, Osho, Swami Vivekanand, Stephen Covey, Jack Welsch and many others.

I also would like to acknowledge the inputs received from Osho publications on various chapters.

Preface

On a hot July day, during my visit to Paris, my friend Margot and I were out for a walk on the streets of the city. After long distance, our conversation shifted to the work-life balance and how our training programs best help the various professionals achieve it.

Later, sitting in Margot's apartment and sipping a warm cup of tea, I said:

"Of course, everything that the organisations do, have a purpose of getting the effectiveness and better productivity from the team. The individuals do get benefits out of them. But in the process, does anyone, including themselves, care for the overall development of the individuals? Why not look at the people as assets to drive the organisation for business benefits as well as a better society?"

Margot agreed and added:

"The very moment an executive comes back from a training program, his superiors are keen to take immediate business benefits and squeeze the juices out of him. However, the objective should be for overall development of the individual. First look at the long term benefits of investing in overall and holistic development, thus making the individual a stakeholder in a better, larger and healthier society that should care for the planet. But on the contrary, we are chasing only self-centred business interest and want to squeeze the people who arc already over stressed, over worked and over exploited.

Can One Really Squeeze the millions already dry due to stress?

This book talks about how important it is to have the enlightenment, self awareness and holistic development of individual.

Contents

Section I: The Work Life Balance: Myth and Reality

Section II: Is there a Way Out in The Stress Jungle?

Section III: Spirituality in Business, The right Way Out

Section I:

Work Life Balance: The Myth and Reality

- 5 Biggest Myths About Work
- The Work Place Diaspora: Are we driven by the technology?
- Coping With Stress in a Stressful Economy
- Managing Pressure At Work
- Seven Stupid Thinking Errors We Make
- Top Ten Unhappy Work Principles!
- How to Avoid Work Burn Outs!

5 Biggest Myths about Work

Myth One: Work leads to retirement

This is the biggest myth of all. First of all, most people simply can no longer afford to stop working. Even for those who do stop working, they soon find that their lives are filled with too much leisure time. Soon a feeling of wanting to make a greater difference in the world will emerge. For most of us, it is the question how can I keep working? It seems that currently the organizations are hiring the youngest workers at the lowest price they can get. Just looking around, it is evident that those over 40 seem to get pushed out sooner than later.

Take Control: After 40, it is mandatory to take control of one's life and work. First, only those who truly don't love their work want to retire. Otherwise why would anyone want to stop doing what they love? Our society sends a strong message for those planning retirement. Despite this, it is mandatory to take responsibility for finding work that last a lifetime.

Money magazine: Money magazine once stressed that it was time to increase the retirement saving. Sure, so others can make money at your expense. I find this advice very misleading and irresponsible. This is like telling people they should save more for their life after their death. When you do what you love, there is no reason to ever stop working. So why save for death?

The education system: Our education system, throughout high school, college, and later adult education rarely teaches us how to discover and do the work you love forever. What can be more important?

What happens when you don't retire?

You start to place a new emphasis on living, especially in the present. You are able to make more choices, take more risks and have more courage with your life and work. Don't fall for the retirement message, its outdated and no longer useful.

Myth Two: Do work you are good at

After 40, often for many people, the work that they are good at no longer brings the same joy as 15 or 20 years ago. You are not the same person at 40 or 50 as you were at 20 or 30. Much has changed. In many cases, the same work no longer provides passion, meaning and fulfilment.

However, there is a tendency to continue to do work which we are good at, even if we are no longer interested. This is a strategy to retirement and quick death. The best way to prolong life is to live fully, each and every day, doing work that makes a difference to you. That will also impact others in a good way. After 40, it is much better to focus around your deep interests and then learn how to do it.

I hear stories all the time from clients, that they would love to do this but don't have the skills. But it turns out that what you are interested in the most you can learn quickly and be good at. Do you find yourself working in areas which others are proud of and you are good at but no longer interested in? It is time to change.

Myth Three: Work is not something to be enjoyed

The historical view is that work should be hard, not enjoyed and not even something one might be good at. This notion has stayed with us.

Even today's career counsellors will nudge people into jobs and careers which the market wants. This is the wrong approach.

First you must start with the work that you enjoy and then build a market around you. I had a client once who loved building model airplanes. For sure, the world didn't rush to his doorstep. Also, he had a family to support and bills to pay. Fast forward 3 years later he owns a model airplane hobby store, rents out the store to Boy Scout groups for adventure days and many related activities which bring in income he needs. Is he rich by society standards? Probably not, but he pays his bills and he might live longer. Are you working in an area you don't enjoy? It is time to change – no excuses!

Myth Four: Work is for only making money

I hear this one all the time. Work after forty has nothing to do with making money at a deep level. Work has to do with feelings of self worth, contribution, deep happiness and a sense that your life matters. Also, work has the opportunity to pay your bills and living expenses. It is a nice combination.

One should never confuse work and money. The best work is when it feels voluntary and the worse work is when it feels obligatory. Of course, one needs to make money but the question is how to make money and live a life which feels fulfilling. There are many ways to make money. The more important question is what will you make money at and where will it lead you? If the answer is retirement, then it is time to change direction.

Myth Five: A resume is necessary and sufficient

This is necessary only because the shallow way we have approached work in our education and thinking. The resume covers only an external view of what you have done. This form doesn't cover your dreams, plans, goals and deep desires when it comes to work. At least the Vita (usually reserved for college professors) gives one the opportunity to discuss what they are most proud of along with current and planned activities.

More important is to develop another document. This is your future biography. I suggest that you write in second person describing the life you wish to live focused around the work you want to do. 2-3 years is a good timeframe. Then you will see the gap and the way to closing it. At least, by the time you write a resume, it will truly reflect the direction you most want to take. The resume is necessary but it is not sufficient.

I'll do anything!

Recently a man in the audience in a talk said with arms crossed, "I have been out of work for several years and at this point I'll do anything".

This is not a good strategy for work. It is better to take a moment off and figure out your life's plan around work and then pursue it rather than wasting away time applying for just jobs. Don't fall into the top 5 myths for yourself.

As a result your life will be fuller, happier, and more coherent.

I'll be cheering you on as you go!

The Workplace Diaspora

Two Managers in the Modern Workplace

Arun is a modern manager. Based at Bangalore, he works for a food company that supplies products across the globe. Same is the case with his colleague Mukesh. They work in various shifts to manage the customers from different parts and the time zones. Recently both of them faced an axe on their jobs following poor performance, cost cutting measures and not being efficient to deal with the stress levels.

The Workplace Diaspora

While Arun and Mukesh's cases might seem extreme, they're not all that unusual. We hear about the world being "flatter" and "24X7", but what do those terms really mean? The implications affect workers nearly every day in ways large and small:

- WebEx, the world's best known web conferencing platform estimates that they hold 50,000 web meetings a day, 7 days a week and has over 2 Million subscribers
- According to Citrix, 23% of America's white-collar workers work at least one day a week from a location other than their office, and 60% would like the option
- Research in the UK suggests that at any time, nearly a third of the desks in offices in the City of London are empty, because people are working from home, visiting branch offices of their company or out on customer sites
- By some estimates, 70% of middle managers around the world have at least one direct report who doesn't work in the same office or general location they do. The old concept of "management by walking around" doesn't apply when, as one manager put it, "It's a long walk to Mumbai".

According to the American Society for Training and Development (ASTD), companies in the US spend about $1,425 US per employee for training. With a larger percentage of that budget threatened by travel and lost opportunity costs, the alternative is to blow out travel budgets or reduce the amount of training per employee. No wonder then that alternatives such as on-line learning and synchronous web-based training (webinars, online coaching) are becoming more popular.

For the first time, managers are facing new challenges, with little in the way of reliable best practices to look to for guidance. How do individual managers and their companies manage this workplace diaspora while maintaining their focus on human relationships, training and performance?

Tow managers in the modern workplace

Many managers and their companies are doing the best they can, on an ad hoc basis. We had to look at ways to proxy communication. Increasing the overall volume of email helped a bit – we mandated daily and weekly status reports from each team member. However, we also increased the frequency of our phone conversations and started using collaboration tools like Skype and Mitel. Seeing one of your team members that you never met smiling at you over their webcam and talking about their work face-to face is a great way to build trust and accountability.

Low-cost (and even free tools) like Skype are just some ideas that the one way managers use for stepping up and finding innovative solutions. Mukesh and Arun's experiences are not unique, and they both point to something that can complicate cross continental training and communication efforts – the human factor.

Technology is the Answer-Right?

There is a tendency in the business to believe that the answer to all ills is to be found in IT solutions. Classroom training can be replaced by online solutions. People don't have to get together – web meetings (also known as web conferencing) are getting increasingly popular. For our purposes, we'll assume they're the same thing. Conference calls, email and Instant Messaging enable people to connect just as well without having to get them on an airplane or wasting time in traffic. Just raise the IT budget and get out of the way.

Communication is not simply the flow of data. Information Technology does that exceptionally well. It's a complicated process of interpretation that involves the "3 V"s (verbal, vocal and visual information).

Arun explains some of the challenges he faced in trying to work with his team. "Conference calls and video conferences work fine when you are simply discussing something but many of our internal meetings need shared data (working on sales forecasts) or shared screen (Systems training or presentations) or even just shared meeting minutes. Emailing updates every 10 minutes is just painful and always running behind real time."

Frustration, lack of trust and other all-too-human emotional complications can take something that looks simple on the surface and render it useless. Worse, it can build resentment and frustration to a point where information still flows through the pipe, though there just may be nothing to communicate.

Not only that, but the competing needs of the Business, IT and the various departments can create logjams and poor decisions that impact the effectiveness of communication in the long run.

Let's start with the human component and bring it down to the company or implementation level.

The Richness to Scope Ratio and Why It Matters

When it comes to quality of communication, a simple model will show why technology plays such an important role. According to the research, all communication is a balance of "Richness" (the multiple real-time ways we gather and interpret communication) and "Scope" (how quickly, consistently and widely a message can be disseminated).

A face-to-face meeting between two people is incredibly "rich" – as two people speak, you get the undivided attention of the listener, you both can hear not only the words used, but the tone of voice, rate of speech, body language and other non-verbal communication that adds context. Because there are only two of you, the conversation happens in real time- you can interrupt, ask clarifying questions and connect on a human level. The message is as clear and undiluted as possible. Rich, indeed.

On the other hand, a manager would be hard pressed to have a face to face meeting every time with every employee – especially if they are separated by continents. How do you address that challenge? There are plenty of tools that help increase the "scope".

Email, for example allows you to send the same message at the same time to thousands of people anywhere in the world. That's the good news. As anyone who has ever spent two days explaining what they really meant when they sent an email because of the lack of interactivity and context ("I was just kidding" being only one source of confusion), these messages become less rich as scope increases. Misunderstandings will inevitably arise without the opportunity to question, clarify and get answers to questions quickly.

If we think about all the ways companies can communicate over distances, the different tools fall like this on the Richness vs. Scope matrix:

Why should companies take this scale into account when planning to overcome distance in the workplace?

Consider the impact of choosing the wrong tool in a few specific instances.

Team cohesion and communication

Arun and Mukesh have discovered that communication tools by themselves don't overcome the human issues that naturally arise during the course of work.

Arun knows this very well from his experience with the team "Phone and video conferences are now common, but have the same challenges. Training remotely can work if you're fine tuning skilled users, but with newcomers it can be slow and painful."

When information is only one-way, scope increases but richness decreases. Some of the impacts include:

- Trust diminishes as richness decreases. This can create long-term problems in communication and even result in project cost overruns and team turnover
- Rework increases as the opportunities for confirming assumptions and asking questions decreases
- Research at DePaul University in Chicago shows that when virtual-only tools are used, there is a slight increase in "negative behaviours." These include lying, omitting important behaviour and even bullying-behaviours that are normally held in check by the reality of human interaction. If you don't have to look someone in the eye and receive rich feedback, there are fewer checks on these bad behaviours.

Training and choosing the right tools

One area where this richness vs. scope discussion really hits home is when the wrong tool is chosen to deliver training.

Remember that there are several reasons companies train their employees:

- To ensure tasks are done correctly

- To help all employees perform at least to minimal acceptable standards
- To ensure consistency of approach across the organization – people will do the same task the same way

What the companies call training covers a wide spectrum of subjects, from simple data points (this is the form you use for expenses) to higher level, complex processes. Without going into Performance Improvement theory, there are three areas that the training tries to address:

Knowledge (do they know what to do?), **Skill** (can they do it?) and **Attitude** (if they know how, why aren't they doing it?).

In order to use the right approach for the right challenge, the richness vs. scope matrix comes into play.

Getting people together in the classroom to show them a new form to use (a knowledge problem) is overkill – simple transfer of new data doesn't need to be that rich, and it can be accomplished by email or asynchronous, web-based training that can be accessed any time.

Conversely, anyone who has tried to get a team to use a new software application knows that the problem is complex. There are knowledge issues (what is the tool and how does it work?) as well as skill problems (knowing how it works is different from being able to actually input data in an efficient manner) and attitude challenges (the old system worked just fine, why change what isn't broken?).

Addressing skill and attitude issues is impossible without the rich communication that allows you to assess skills, knowledge and attitude, address different learning styles and test whether the **new skill has actually been learned. In a classroom you can tell when someone has a glazed, distracted look. Online, that person could be answering email. How do you know?**

Choosing the right tool and communication method is critical to avoid wasting time and precious resources. After all, putting one hundred people on a web meeting and making them passively watch a demonstration is a waste of everyone's time if at the end they can't actually use the program properly. Your team will spend more time in re-training and helpdesk support than you saved on the training.

In the case of application training, while the temptation is to use something with wide scope and less richness (pre-recorded web-based training or web meetings with multiple participants and a one-way delivery of information), an old-fashioned training approach would dictate small groups with application sharing and a chance for people to actually use the tool and demonstrate they have learned how to use it. In a web-enabled world, this might mean small online groups, using tools like application sharing, chat and other tools. It would take longer to accomplish your goals, but the result will be people actually knowing how to use the application.

An initial investment of time and resources will mean fewer panicky calls to the help desk and faster ramp-up to actually use of the tool your company has invested so much money in.

Mukesh and Arun's solutions

Because both these managers have made careers of being cost-conscious and proactive, they took the initial steps themselves.

Mukesh uses the tools at Portico's disposal like email, IM and telephone. He also uses free services such as Skype and Mitel which used Voice Over IP (VOIP) and cheap web cameras. By making smart decisions about which tool to use when, and choosing the right balance of richness and scope, he's improved the mood of this team as well as their productivity.

If there was one word that summarizes what is working for us now, it would be communication. As much as our schedules allow, we are in touch with our remote team members. We are always forwarding email, Skyping, talking on conference calls and generally interacting with each other as much as we can. It is not always effective, but we have found that one of the ways to build trust with someone on the other side of the world is to increase the frequency of communication. It's not always about work, either; I love to ask someone on the other end of a Skype call what the weather is like where they are, what time it is there and how their weekend went. These human connections, enhanced by technology, pay dividends for the Portico Systems.

Arun has taken a different approach. He uses the low-cost web meeting platform, Dimdim, to hold web meetings for small issues that require interaction and rich communication but aren't worth incurring huge travel and time costs. It allows him to share information, use webcams and voice. It also encourage collaboration using flash video, meaning no plug-ins or other software installation is needed - a real bugbear for many companies. While it is still early days, the results are encouraging and senior management is following events closely.

The role of the company

Individual managers like Arun are taking the initiative where they can. Executive Management doesn't want to hear excuses. They don't want to hear about challenges. They want solutions and on-time results. It was up to the front-line managers to come up with an engagement strategy that worked and that got those results. Kudos to the Executive Managers for believing in the Front Line managers and giving them the tools and the time needed to create that strategy and it couldn't have done without their support.

It's not always that simple, though. The fact that many of these tools require input or approval from Senior Management with budget responsibility, IT and other departments means a holistic approach is required.

Arun encountered some resistance from the IT department because of security concerns. "IT guys are very security and stability conscious. They were not at all keen on the internet based solutions having access to internal data or third parties having access into a hole in our firewall. Their preference is to have an application inside the firewall which has functionality (sharing of files/desktops) restricted to internal meetings".

Without being able to hitch this project onto the bigger one, it would have been a hard struggle to get it approved. You have to show ROI – for example 10 trips from Bangalore to Sydney at $3,000 a trip. This is much easier than trying to quantify how much improvement in the forecast was due to remote teams being able to see the numbers and the amount of profit.

Because there are legitimate concerns from many departments, it's important that companies develop a communication technology strategy. Some of the things they need to consider:

- What are the specific communication challenges your company faces?
- What tools do you already have in your organization to address those challenges?
- What is the cost of not implementing these solutions (lost opportunities, project delays)?
- What training challenges do companies face and where do they fall on the richness vs. scope matrix?

Every part of the organization needs to be involved in these discussions and understand the needs of the other parts. One well-known U.S. bank's international training initiatives are currently stalled because the IT department purchased a solution that won't do what the training department needs it to do – and they are stalled over whether to "make do with what they have" or to find a new solution. Meanwhile tens of thousands of dollars of process and application training is delayed. This situation is not unusual.

Once an organization identifies the tools necessary to meet their communication needs, there is one last question to be addressed: how confident are you that the people (managers, trainers, subject matter experts, sales people) who will use these tools are comfortable with them and fluent in their use? What plans are in place for the training of managers in what will be a core competency in the 21st century.

Investment in a robust web meeting platform like WebEx or LiveMeeting is not going to reap returns if people are uncomfortable using it. Do time-strapped managers use email by default without considering the long term implications of non-rich communication? Do managers insist on breaking the budget because of a preference for one tool over another?

While proactive managers like Mukesh and Arun are great role models, many managers are unfamiliar with the technology or even which tool to use for which challenge. Whether it's technophobia or just unfamiliarity, without integrating these tools with management training and following proven best practices, they will not achieve the cost and time efficiencies that can make them such a powerful tool to companies.

Coping in a Stressful Economy

How to Get a Grip on Stress in a Stressful Economy

If you haven't lost your job, you worry that you will. And while you wait, you've seen your workload increase, your downtimes vanish and your duties expand beyond your expertise (and any conceivable 40-hour week). If all that's not enough to make your blood pressure rise, a new business school study shows that bosses have become more demanding and that politicking, sucking up and backstabbing in the office are on the rise.

Stress test? The office these days is giving you your own personal version, and, in short, you're barely passing.

Stop and take a few deep breaths. In, out. OK? Now read this. You'll feel better.

Understand Stress

Goal: Pinpoint where the anxiety is coming from.

A certain amount of daily stress is normal. Stress, after all, is simply your reaction — either positive or negative — to change, according to the Gale Encyclopedia of Medicine. When stress places prolonged or extreme pressure on your coping mechanisms, it can become a clinical problem that requires professional help. Continually high levels of stress can wreak havoc on the digestive and nervous systems, leading to irritable bowel syndrome, recurrent headaches, and heart attacks. The psychological symptoms often come in the form of burnout (losing interest in work) and depression. The tips below are designed to help you prevent stress from taking a serious toll on your health — and your career.

There are two leading, complementary perspectives on the sources of workplace stress. Understanding the difference between the two is the first step in learning how to cope.

Internal: Stress comes from how you perceive your situation. The very thoughts you have can worsen your stress reaction. For example, one day your boss emerges from a long, closed-door meeting looking upset. Then the boss e-mails you requesting a meeting. Do you immediately think you're facing the axe? "Your mind starts spinning a catastrophe, and it's enough to trigger your body to go into a stress reaction".

Coping Strategy: You may not be able to eliminate the stimulus, but you can learn to change your response and calm your mind. Start keeping a list of everything in your day that causes stress. Is there something new or different in your work life? Do certain colleagues make your blood boil? Pinpoint how every item on the list makes you feel and then ask yourself, "Is my reaction appropriate or over the top?" This step is key, because once you understand where your emotions are coming from, you can find a healthier way to deal with them.

External: This school of thought holds that outside factors, like toxic work environments predominantly drives workplace stress. Common characteristics of stress-inducing environments include authoritarian or

non-communicative supervisors, socially isolating work and jobs that require a lot of effort but offer little reward. These factors can produce biological responses such as higher blood pressure and could possibly contribute to more serious conditions like heart attacks and depression.

Coping strategy: Eliminating the source of the problem (i.e., finding another job) may be the most effective solution in the long term. But until the job market improves, find ways to regain a sense of control over your time and your surroundings. For example, if you must endure a two-hour commute in rush-hour traffic to arrive at the office by 9 a.m., start your workday earlier so you avoid the worst time to travel. If you can't stand your colleagues, shut your office door or take your work to a conference room for part of the day.

Go Ahead and Vent but Find the Right Listener

Goal: Blow off steam without damaging your reputation at work.

Understanding how stress works will only get you so far. You need cathartic relief, right? Don't hesitate to seek the empathetic ears of a colleague, but do choose your confidant wisely. The more you say to a person you work with, the more likely something will slip out at work. You don't want co-workers using your misery to their advantage, so find someone with a sterling reputation whom you know and trust.

As counterintuitive as it sounds, in some cases your boss may be your best confidant. Sure, you don't want to make much ado about the minor, daily stresses of your job, but if you're struggling with something major that affects your performance, talk to your boss. After all, managers are invested in the success of their employees. A brief explanation (keep the hairy details to a minimum) is not only fair, it's also a way to build trust.

One district manager at a global pharmaceutical company recently survived a round of layoffs. Still reeling from the stress of nearly losing his own job, he faced the task of cutting 20 percent of his own employees, many of whom he had worked with for more than 20 years. He asked his former and current bosses for advice because both of them had been through the same experience. The two empathized but, more importantly, offered some concrete tips on how to make the cuts and give employees the support they need. The conversations didn't make the task any easier, but they did help the manager cope with his own internal struggles.

If you're going to go to your boss, schedule a time to talk instead of dropping by unexpectedly when they may be in the middle of grappling with the demands of their own job. Regardless of whom you talk to, vent once and then let the issue rest. Constantly rehashing the story will force you to relive your emotions.

Don't want to vent? Relieve some tension and clear your head by doing something physical. Wear yourself out on the treadmill, go on a strenuous hike, do laps in the swimming pool – whatever you need to do. The activity will get your endorphins pumping (the brain chemicals that make us feel good) and focus your mind on your body instead of your stress.

Learn to Change Your Reaction to Stress

Goal: Stop being tyrannized by your emotions.

After you've blown off some steam, you can work through stress in a more logical, clearheaded way rather than making decisions based on emotions. Don't just be lost in negative feelings.

Rethink your standards: If your failure to achieve perfection causes continual guilt and frustration, redefine what success means. For example, if you always feel inundated with work, ask yourself if you're spending more time on tasks than they require. We actually shoot ourselves in the foot by making the task harder than it needs to be.

Reframe your situation: Weather delays your flight to an important business meeting. Instead of stewing about the disruption to your schedule, which you can't control anyway, take advantage of the extra time to prepare for your presentation or catch up on sleep.

Reassess the significance of the problem: Will it matter tomorrow? Next week? A year from now? Emotion magnifies the difficulty of a problem in the moment; perspective shrinks it. So make sure you give yourself a steady dose of the latter.

Things you will need:

Time: Start setting aside enough hours for a full night's sleep, plus extra time each week for tension-relieving activities and self-reflection.

Social support: Single out a few good friends and family members to lean on. Research shows that when lonely people are stressed, they experience higher blood pressure and more insomnia than those who have a strong social network.

Self-awareness: Don't avoid the problem. That will only make it worse. Failure to change your surroundings or manage your stress level can contribute to long-term health issues like clinical depression, anxiety disorder, and heart disease.

Managing Pressure at Work

For many people, being part of the business world comes at a substantial personal cost: stress. People often say this is a part of a high pressure job, as if this testifies to the position's prestige. However, for the people whose ability to cope is at a crisis point, stress is no longer a matter of bravado. For them, stress is a serious problem that can have far-reaching consequences. To avoid reaching this point, stress must be managed.

What You Need to Know

My supervisor gets a real buzz from being under pressure and so assumes I do too.

However, I much prefer working in a calmer environment. Is there a way we can work well together?

This happens frequently, but the good news is that your differing styles can actually complement each other. Raise the subject with your boss and suggest that you discuss to create a plan of action. However, you may still find it easiest to limit the contact with your boss while working on joint projects.

I enjoy working under pressure, but it is starting to affect my relationships with others. What should I do?

It can be true that a hovering deadline gives us the adrenaline boost we need to get a job done well and promptly. But if working in this way becomes a habit, it's easy for it to become the norm. While people can become very focused in such an environment, other areas of their lives, such as time spent with friends and family, may be neglected. Their heath may also suffer as a result. In the long term, pressure should not have a permanent place in anyone's working life, but if you feel it is becoming part of your organization's preferred way of working, flag it up.

How do I exploit the benefits of pressure while diminishing the downside?

Pressure can raise our performance, but sometimes at the detriment of other factors, such as relationships. Under pressure, some people become highly task-oriented, focusing on immediate areas. Others become very short-term oriented. Explore what happens to you, seek feedback and evaluate whether you believe there is an issue or not. The earlier you recognize it, the easier it is to ensure that the negative impact of pressure is alleviated.

What to Do

Know the Symptoms of Stress

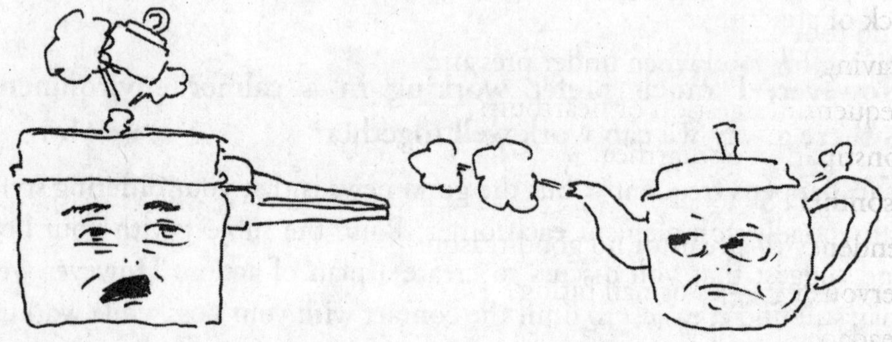

It is important to be able to distinguish between pressure and stress. Pressure is motivating, stimulating, and energizing. But when pressure exceeds our ability to cope, stress is produced. Sustained high levels of stress can, at worst, result in illness, depression, or even nervous breakdown. However, there are a number of warning signs that can help you determine when your level of stress is bordering on dangerous.

Take a good look at your well-being. If you experience some of the following behavioral and physical symptoms on a frequent or near-constant basis, it can indicate that you have crossed the line between healthy pressure and harmful stress.

Behavioral symptoms

Constant irritability with people
Difficulty in making decisions

Loss of sense of humour
Suppressed anger
Difficulty concentrating
Inability to finish one task before rushing into another
Feeling the target of other people's animosity
Feeling unable to cope
Wanting to cry at the smallest problem
Lack of interest in doing things after returning home from work
Waking up in the morning and feeling tired after an early night
Constant tiredness

Physical symptoms

Lack of appetite
Craving for food when under pressure
Frequent indigestion or heartburn
Constipation or diarrhea
Insomnia
Tendency to sweat for no good reason
Nervous twitches or nail biting
Headaches
Cramps and muscle spasms
Nausea
Breathlessness without exertion
Constant tiredness
Fainting spells
Impotency or frigidity
Eczema

Identify Sources of Stress in the Workplace

If you feel that you are not coping well with the everyday pressures at work, creating an action plan to cut down (or cut out altogether) excess pressure is the next sensible step. To do that, identify the sources of workplace stress you face. For example, it could be that you're struggling with some of the following:

Trouble with client/customer
Too much travel
Having to work late
Constant people interruptions
Conflict with organizational goals
Trouble with boss
Job interfering with home/family life
Deadlines and time pressures
Overflowing in-box
Telephone interruptions
Difficult decision-making
Dealing with the bureaucracy at work
Not enough stimulating things to do
Too many meetings
Trouble with co-workers
Uncertainty about career direction
Worried about job security
Too much responsibility
Unsupportive spouse/partner
Too many jobs to do at once
Long commute

In addition to these potential daily hassles, there are, of course, more significant problem areas. These may include coping with lay-offs, dealing with a bullying boss, or trying to cope with a dysfunctional corporate culture that demands excessive working hours or employs an autocratic management style.

Strive for Work-Life Balance

Managing pressure is often about achieving some balance between work and the rest of your life. It is usually in the workplace that we are most susceptible to pressure, but it can also stem from a home or social environment. Avoid allowing work to become the central focus of your life. For example, take advantage of your vacation time, exercise regularly and maintain relationships with friends and family. Practicing hobbies the mind – and then these things happen. And remember, you may not murder, but your continuous thinking of murdering somebody may create the situation in which the person is murdered. Somebody may take your thought, because there are weaker persons all around and thoughts flow like water: downwards. If you think something continuously, someone who is a weakling may take your thought and go and kill a person.

That's why those who have known the inner reality of man say that whatsoever happens on the earth, everybody is responsible. Everybody. Whatsoever happens in Vietnam, not only are the Nixons responsible, everybody who thinks is also responsible. Only one person can not be held responsible, and that is the person who has no mind; otherwise everybody is responsible for everything that goes on. If the earth is a hell, you are a creator, you participate.

Don't go on throwing responsibility on others – you are also responsible, it is a collective phenomenon. The disease may bubble up anywhere, the explosion may happen millions, thousands of miles away from you – that doesn't make any difference, because thought is a non-spatial phenomenon, it needs no space.

That's why it travels fastest. Even light cannot travel so fast, because even for light space is needed. Thought travels fastest. In fact it takes no time in travelling, space doesn't exist for it. You may be here, thinking of something, and it happens in America. How can you be held responsible? No court can punish you, but in the ultimate court of existence you will be punished – you are already punished. That's why you are so miserable.

People come to me and they say: "We never do anything wrong to anybody, and still we are so miserable." You may not be doing, you may be thinking – and thinking is more subtle than doing.

A person can protect himself from doing, but he cannot protect himself from thinking. For thinking everybody is vulnerable.

No-thinking is a must if you want to be completely freed from sin, freed from crime, freed from all that goes around you – and that is the meaning of a buddha.

A buddha is a person who lives without the mind; then he is not responsible. That's why in the east we say that he never accumulates karma; he never accumulates any entanglements for the future. He lives, he walks, he moves, he eats, he talks, he is doing many things, so he must accumulate karma, because karma means activity. But in the east it is said even if a buddha kills, he will not accumulate karma. Why? And you, even if you don't kill, you will accumulate karma. Why?

It is simple: whatsoever buddha is doing, he is doing without any mind in it. He is spontaneous, it is not activity. He is not thinking about it, it happens. He is not the doer. He moves like an emptiness. He has no mind for it, he was not thinking to do it. But if the existence allows it to happen, he allows it to happen. He has no more the ego to resist; no more the ego to do.

That is the meaning of being empty and a no-self: just being a non-being, anatta, no-selfness. Then you accumulate nothing; then you are not responsible for anything that goes on around you; then you transcend.

Each single thought is creating something for you and for others. Be alert!

But when I say be alert, I don't mean that think good thoughts, no, because whenever you think good thoughts, by the side you are also thinking of bad thoughts. How can good exist without bad? If you think of love, just by the side, behind it, is hidden hate. How can you think about love without thinking about hate? You may not think consciously, love may be in the conscious layer of the mind, but hate is hidden in the unconscious – they move together.

Whenever you think of compassion, you think of cruelty. Can you think of compassion without thinking of cruelty? Can you think of non-violence without thinking of violence? In the very word "non-violence," violence enters; it is there in the very concept. Can you think of brahmacharya, celibacy, without thinking of sex? It is impossible, because what will celibacy mean if there is no thought of sex? And if brahmacharya is based on the thought of sex, what type of brahmacharya is this?

No, there is a totally different quality of being which comes by not thinking: not good, not bad, simply a state of no-thinking. You simply watch, you simply remain conscious, but you don't think. And if some thought enters...it will enter, because thoughts are not yours; they are just floating in the air. All around there is a noosphere, a thoughtsphere, all around. Just as there is air, there is thought all around you, and it goes on entering on its own accord. It stops only when you become more and more aware. There is something in it: if you become more aware, a thought simply disappears, it melts, because awareness is a greater energy than thought.

Awareness is like fire to thought.

It is just like you burn a lamp in the house and the darkness cannot enter; you put the light off – from everywhere darkness has entered; without taking a single minute, a single moment, it is there. When the light burns in the house, the darkness cannot enter. Thoughts are like darkness: they enter only if there is no light within. Awareness is fire: you become more aware, less and less thoughts enter.

If you become really integrated in your awareness, thoughts don't enter you; you have become an impenetrable citadel, nothing can penetrate you. Not that you are closed, remember – you are absolutely open; but just the very energy of awareness becomes your citadel. And when no thoughts can enter you, they will come and they will bypass you. You will see them coming, and simply, by the time they reach near you they turn. Then you can move anywhere, then you go to the very hell – nothing can affect you. This is what we mean by enlightenment.

Sometimes you see in a madman's eyes an empty look – and madmen and sages are alike in certain things. A madman looks at your face, but you can see he is not looking at you. He just looks through you as if you are a glass thing, transparent; you are just in the way, he is not looking at you. And you are transparent for him: he looks beyond you, through you. He looks without looking at you; the "at" is not present, he simply looks.

Look in the sky without looking for something, because if you look for something a cloud is bound to come: "something" means a cloud, "nothing" means the vast expanse of the blue sky. Don't look for any object. If you look for an object, the very look creates the object: a cloud comes, and then you are looking at a cloud. Don't look at the clouds. Even if there are clouds, you don't look at them – simply look, let them float, they are there. Suddenly a moment comes when you are attuned to this look of not-looking – clouds disappear for you, only the vast sky remains. It is difficult because eyes are focused and your eyes are tuned to look at things.

Look at a small child the first day born. He has the same eyes as a sage – or like a madman: his eyes are loose and floating. He can bring both his eyes to meet at the center; he can allow them to float to the far corners – they are not yet fixed. His system is liquid, his nervous system is not yet a structure, everything is floating. So a child looks without looking at things; it is a mad look. Watch a child: the same look is needed from you, because again you have to attain a second childhood.

Watch a madman, because the madman has fallen out of the society. Society means the fixed world of roles, games. A madman is mad because he has no fixed role now, he has fallen out: he is the perfect drop-out. A sage is also a perfect drop-out in a different dimension. He is not mad; in fact he is the only sanest possibility. But the whole world is mad, fixed – that's why a sage also looks mad. Watch a madman: that is the look which is needed.

In old schools of Tibet they always had a madman, just for the seekers to watch his eyes.

A madman was very much valued. He was searched after because a monastery could not exist without a madman. He becomes an object to observe. The seekers will observe the madman, his eyes, and then they will try to look at the world like the madman. Those days were beautiful.

In the east, madmen have never suffered like they are suffering in the west. In the east they were valued, a madman was something special. The society took care of him, he was respected, because he has certain elements of the sage, certain elements of the child.

He is different from the so-called society, culture, civilization; he has fallen out of it. Of course, he has fallen down; a sage falls up, a madman falls down – that's the difference – but both have fallen out. And they have similarities. Watch a madman, and then try to let your eyes become unfocused.

In Harvard, they were doing one experiment a few years ago, and they were surprised, they couldn't believe it. They were trying to find out whether the world, as we see it, is so or not – because many things have surfaced within the few last years.

We see the world not as it is, we see it as we expect it to be seen, we project something onto it.

It happened that a great ship reached a small island in the pacific for the first time. The people of the island didn't see it, nobody! And the ship was so vast – but the people were attuned, their eyes were attuned to small boats. They had never known such a big ship, they had never seen such a thing. Simply their eyes would not catch the glimpse, their eyes simply refused.

In Harvard they tried it on a young man: they gave him spectacles with distorting glasses, and he had to wear them for seven days. For the first three days he was in a miserable state, because everything was distorted, the whole world around him was distorted.... It gave him such a severe headache, he couldn't sleep. Even with closed eyes those distorted figures would be there...the faces distorted, the trees distorted, the roads distorted. He couldn't even walk because he couldn't believe: "What is true and what is given by the projection of distorting glasses?" But a miracle happened! After the third day he became attuned to it; the distortion disappeared. The glasses remained the same, distorting, but he started looking at the world in the same old way. Within a week everything was okay: there was no headache, no problem, and the scientists were simply surprised; they couldn't believe it was happening. The eyes had completely dropped, as if the glasses were no longer there. The glasses were there, and they were distorting – but the eyes had come to see the world for which they were trained.

Nobody knows whether what you are seeing is there or not. It may not be there, it may be there in a totally different way. The colours you see, the forms you see, everything is projected by the eyes. And whenever you look fixedly, focused with your old patterns, you see things according to your own conditioning. That's why a madman has a liquid look, an absent look, looking and not looking together.

This look is beautiful. It is one of the greatest tantra techniques:

If one sees naught when staring into space...

Don't see, just look. For the beginning few days, again and again you will see something, just because of the old habit. We hear things because of old habit. We see things because of old habit. We understand things because of old habit.

One of the greatest disciples of Gurdjieff, P.D. Ouspensky, used to insist on a certain thing with his disciples – and everybody resented it, and many people left simply because of that insistence. If somebody said: "Yesterday you told..." he immediately would stop him and say: "don't say it like that. Say: 'I understood that you said this thing yesterday.' 'I understood....' don't say what I said; you cannot know that. Talk about what you heard." And he would insist so much because we are habitual.

Again you might say: "In the Bible it is said..." and he would say: "Don't say that! Simply say that you understand that this is said in the Bible." With each sentence he insisted: "Always remember that this is your understanding."

We go on forgetting. His disciples went on forgetting again and again, and every day, and he was stubborn about it. He would not allow you to go on. He would say: "go back. Say first that: 'I understand you said this, this is my understanding'...because you hear according to yourself, you see according to yourself – because you have a fixed pattern of seeing and hearing."

This has to be dropped. To know existence, all fixed attitudes have to be dropped. Your eyes should be just windows, not projectors. Your ears should be just doors, not projectors.

It happened: one psychoanalyst who was studying with Gurdjieff tried to do this experiment. In a wedding ceremony he tried a very simple but beautiful experiment. He stood by the side, people passing, and he watched them and he felt that nobody at the receiving end was hearing what they were saying – so many people, some rich man's wedding ceremony.

So he also joined in and he said very quietly to the first person in the receiving line: "My grandmother died today." The man said: "So good of you, so beautiful." Then to another he said it and the man said: "How nice of you." And to the groom, when he said this, he said: "Old man, it is time you also followed."

Nobody is listening to anybody. You hear whatsoever you expect. Expectation is your specs – that is the glasses. Your eyes should be windows – this is the technique.

Nothing should go out of the eyes, because if something goes a cloud is created. Then you see things which are not there, then a subtle hallucination.... Let pure clarity be in the eyes, in the ears; all your senses should be clear, perception pure – only then the existence can be revealed to you. And when you know existence, then you know that you are a Buddha, a god, because in existence everything is divine.

If one sees naught when staring into space;
if with the mind one then observes the mind...

First stare into the sky; lie down on the ground and just stare at the sky. Only one thing has to be tried: don't look at anything. In the beginning you will fall again and again, you will forget again and again. You will not be able to remember continuously. Don't be frustrated, it is natural because of so long a habit. Whenever you remember again, unfocus your eyes, make them loose, just look at the sky – not doing anything, just looking. Soon a time comes when you can see into the sky without trying to see anything there.

Then try it with your inner sky:

...If with the mind one then observes the mind...

Then close your eyes and look inside, not looking for anything, just the same absent look. Thoughts floating but you are not looking for them, or at them – you are simply looking. If they come it is good, if they don't come it is good also. Then you will be able to see the gaps: one thought passes, another comes – and the gap. And then, by and by, you will be able to see that the thought becomes transparent, even when the thought is passing you continue to see the gap, you continue to see the hidden sky behind the cloud.

And the more you get attuned to this vision, thoughts will drop by and by, they will come less and less, less and less. The gaps will become wider. For minutes together no thought coming, everything is so quiet and silent inside – you are for the first time together. Everything feels absolutely blissful, no disturbance. And if this look becomes natural to you – it becomes, it is one of the most natural things; one just has to unfocus, decondition:

...One destroys distinctions...
Then there is nothing good, nothing bad;
nothing ugly, nothing beautiful.
...And reaches buddhahood.

Buddhahood means the highest awakening. When there are no distinctions, all divisions are lost, unity is attained, only one remains. You cannot even call it "one," because that too is part of duality. One remains, but you cannot call it "one," because how can you call it "one" without deep down saying "two." No, you don't say that "one" remains, simply that "two" has disappeared, the many has disappeared. Now it is a vast oneness, there are no boundaries to anything.

One tree merging into another tree, earth merging into the trees, trees merging into the sky, the sky merging into the beyond...you merging in me, I merging in you...everything merging...distinctions lost, melting and merging like waves into other waves...a vast oneness vibrating, alive, without boundaries, without definitions, without distinctions...the sage merging into the sinner, the sinner merging into the sage...good becoming bad, bad becoming good...night turning into the day, the day turning into the night...life melting into death, death moulding again into life – then everything has become one.

Only at this moment is Buddhahood attained: when there is nothing good, nothing bad, no sin, no virtue, no darkness, no night – nothing, no distinctions. Distinctions are there because of your trained eyes. Distinction is a learned thing. Distinction is not there in existence. Distinction is projected by you. Distinction is given by you to the world – it is not there. It is your eyes' trick, your eyes playing a trick on you.

The clouds that wander through the sky have no roots, no home; nor do the distinctive thoughts floating through the mind. Once the self-mind is seen, discrimination stops.

The clouds that wander through the sky have no roots, no home... And the same is true for your thoughts, and the same is true for your inner sky. Your thoughts have no roots, they have no home; they wander just like clouds. So you need not fight them, you need not be against them, you need not even try to stop thought.

This should become a deep understanding in you, because whenever a person becomes interested in meditation he starts trying to stop thinking. And if you try to stop thoughts they will never be stopped, because the very effort to stop is a thought, the very effort to meditate is a thought, the very effort to attain buddhahood is a thought. And how can you stop a thought by another thought? How can you stop mind by creating another mind? Then you will be clinging to the other. And this will go on and on, ad nauseam; then there is no end to it.

Don't fight – because who will fight? Who are you? Just a thought, so don't make yourself a battle ground of one thought fighting another. Rather, be a witness, you just watch thoughts floating. They stop, but not by your stopping. They stop by your becoming more aware, not by any effort on your part to stop them. No, they never stop, they resist. Try and you will find: try to stop a thought and the thought will persist. Thoughts are very stubborn, adamant; they are hath yogis, they persist. You throw them away and they will come back a million and one times. You will get tired, but they will not get tired.

And this is in fact the case. When you think you are tinged, it is just thinking. When you think that you have become good or bad, sinner or sage, it is just thinking, because your inner sky never becomes anything – it is a being, it never becomes anything. All becoming is just getting identified with some form and name, some colour, some form arising in the space – all becoming. You are a being, you are already that – no need to become anything.

Look at the sky: spring comes and the whole atmosphere is filled with birds singing, and then flowers and the fragrance. And then comes the fall, and then comes summer. Then comes the rain – and everything goes on changing, changing, changing. And it all happens in the sky, but nothing tinges it. It remains deeply distant; everywhere present, and distant; nearest to everything and farthest away.

A sannyasin is just like the sky: he lives in the world – hunger comes, and satiety; summer comes, and winter; good days, bad days; good moods, very elated, ecstatic, euphoric; bad moods, depressed, in the valley, dark, burdened – everything comes and goes and he remains a watcher. He simply looks, and he knows everything will go, many things will come and go. He is no more identified with anything.

Non-identification is *sannyas*, and *sannyas* is the greatest flowering, the greatest blooming that is possible.

In space shapes and colours form, but neither by black nor white is space tinged. From the self-mind all things emerge, the mind by virtues and by vices is not stained.

When Buddha attained to the ultimate, the utterly ultimate enlightenment, he was asked: "What have you attained?" He laughed and said: "Nothing – because whatsoever I have attained was already there inside me. It is not something new that I have achieved. It has always been there from eternity, it is my very nature. But I was not mindful about it, I was not aware of it. The treasure was always there, but I had forgotten about it."

You have forgotten, that's all – that is your ignorance. Between a Buddha and you there is no distinction as far as your nature is concerned, but only one distinction, and that distinction is that you don't remember who you are – and he remembers. You are the same, but he remembers and you don't remember. He is awake, you are fast asleep, but your nature is the same.

Try to live it out in this way – Tilopa is talking about techniques – live in the world as if you are the sky, make it your very style of being. Somebody is angry at you, insulting – watch. If anger arises in you, watch; be a watcher on the hills, go on looking and looking and looking. And just by looking, without looking at anything, without getting obsessed by anything, when your perception becomes clear, suddenly, in a moment, in fact no time happens, suddenly, without time, you are fully awake; you are a Buddha, you become the enlightened, the awakened one.

What does a Buddha gain out of it? He gains nothing. Rather, on the contrary, he loses many things: the misery, the pain, the anguish, the anxiety, the ambition, the jealousy, the hatred, the possessiveness, the violence – he loses all. As far as what he attains, nothing. He attains that which was already there, he remembers.

The Last Luxury

THE LAST LUXURY

In our civilization, professional people like me have a particular problem: we make too much use of our intelligence, so much so that we tend to view life through the intellect only, thus negating all other means of doing so. This tends to make life boring and dull, and robs it of its lustre.

No one can use his intellect too much. It is such a great force, with so much potential, that you cannot use it too much. Not only do you not use it too much, but you never even use it totally. Ordinarily, you do not use more than ten to fifteen percent of your total intellectual potential.

And another thing: when you do intellectual work it does not necessarily mean that you are using your intelligence. Intellectual work, too, is mechanical. Once you acquire the know-how, no intelligence is required at all; the mind works just like a computer.

The real problem is not the use of too much intelligence but the non-use of emotion. Emotion is completely disregarded in our civilization, so the balance is lost and a lopsided personality develops. If emotion is also used, then there is no imbalance.

A balance of emotion and intellect must be maintained in the proper ratio; otherwise the whole personality gets diseased. It is just like using only one leg. You may keep on using it, but you get nowhere; you simply tire yourself. The other leg must be used. Emotion and intellect are like two wings: when we use only one wing the outcome will be frustration. Then the bliss that comes from using both wings simultaneously, in balance and harmony, is never attained.

Don't be afraid of using the intellect too much. Only when intelligence is used do you touch the depths; only there is your potential stimulated. Intellectual work does not mean that your intelligence is being used.

Intellectual work is merely superficial; no depth is touched, nothing is challenged. That gives rise to boredom; it creates work that is without enjoyment. Enjoyment always comes when your individuality is challenged and you have to prove yourself and respond to the challenge. When challenged, intelligence or emotion both create their own bliss.

A person is schizophrenic if only one part of his personality is working and the other is dead. Then even the part that is working will not work really well because it will be overworked. Personality is a totality; it has no division at all. Actually, the whole personality is a flowing energy. When energy is used in a logical way it becomes intelligence, and when it is not used logically but emotionally it becomes the heart. These are two separate things; it is the same energy flowing through two different channels.

When there is no heart but only intellect, you can never relax.

Relaxation means that now the same energy within you is working in a different channel. Relaxation never means no-work, it means work in another dimension. Then the dimension that is overtaxed relaxes.

A person who follows an intellectual pursuit continuously, never relaxes. He does not divert his energy to another dimension, so his mind goes on working in only one direction unnecessarily. That creates boredom. Thoughts and more thoughts come and go; energy is diffused, wasted. You cannot enjoy it; on the contrary, you will be disappointed and disgusted with this unnecessary burden. But the mind, or the intellect, is not at fault. Because an alternative dimension has not been provided, because there is no other door open to it, the energy keeps circling round and round inside you.

Energy can never be stagnant. Energy means that which is not stagnant, that which is always flowing. Relaxation does not mean energy which is stagnant or asleep; scientifically, relaxation means that now energy is flowing through another channel, another dimension – it has entered another room.

But even though the room may be different, if it is not the very opposite of the room you were in before, the mind will not relax. For example, if you work on a scientific problem, then you can relax by reading a novel. The work is different: to deal with a scientific problem is to be active – a very masculine mode – whereas to read a novel is to be passive, which is an absolutely feminine mode.

Even though you are using the same mind you will be relaxed, because it is the opposite pole of the mind which is being used. You are not solving anything, you are not active; you are just a receiver, receiving something. The dimension is the same except that emotion, the opposite pole, is being brought into use.

In the same way, when we love, the intellect does not come into play at all. Quite the opposite happens: the irrational part of your personality comes into action. Intelligence must be balanced by love and love must be balanced by intelligence. Ordinarily, this balance is not found anywhere.

If someone is in love and begins to neglect all intellectual pursuits, this too will create boredom. Even love becomes a tension if it is a twenty-four-hour-a-day affair.

Once the challenge is lost, the enjoyment will also be lost: the play will be lost and it will become just work. The same thing happens with an intellectual who neglects the emotional side of his being.

These two parts, these two poles, must be in balance, only then is an integrated and individuated human being born; otherwise, whether emotional or intellectual, it will be the same disease. The east has become warped because it has been too concerned with the heart, while the west has been too concerned with the opposite pole. Both have achieved disastrous results.

In the west, the new generation is now rebelling against intellect, against reason. The whole mind of the new generation is leaning toward the irrational. Nature always takes its own revenge. Nature is very vengeful: it never pardons, it never forgets. If some part of it remains suppressed or unfulfilled it will have its revenge. In the west the irrational is taking its revenge. In the east the appeal is of the rational, the scientific: communism has much appeal and religion has lost its appeal. The irrational no longer appeals to the east because reason has been suppressed for too long.

To me, neither a human being nor a human culture can be healthy without an inner balance between the rational and the irrational. I do not take them to be two different things. I take them to be two poles of the same energy.

All energy can only exist between two opposite poles; energy requires an inner tension in order to create itself, in order to be. The poles can be negative and positive as in electricity, or north and south as in magnetism, or male and female as in biology, but energy cannot exist at only one pole. The opposite is needed in order to challenge, to stimulate, to create the necessary tension.

But in human society the other pole is always suppressed – either intellect is suppressed or emotion is suppressed.

A total culture has not come into existence yet, because there have only been civilizations of either the intellect or of the emotions. Culture, meaning a civilization in which the two poles function simultaneously, is as yet unborn.

Always balance one pole by its opposite. Then the more one pole is put to use, the more the opposite pole for which it is a relaxation will be illuminated. The mind must be capable of changing from one pole to the opposite pole just as easily as one moves from waking to sleeping. One must be able to be close to one dimension and remain open to the other. When this happens life is no longer dull; it becomes bliss.

Unfortunately, we become addicted to one polarity. Why is there this addiction to one extreme? We become addicted to one way of functioning because we have been trained for it. It is easier – you can function in the way that is familiar to you without any conscious effort – consciousness is not required.

When you change from one pole to the other, when you change your total perspective, you become an amateur. In this other realm you are not an expert; you are not trained in it. When you try to escape from it, then you tend to overburden that realm in which you are proficient.

This overdoing is the problem. One must not be an expert twenty-four hours a day; one must also do something in which one is a no one and about which one knows nothing. One must be a child sometimes: playing, immature, unknowing, ignorant.

Every genius has a child in him; no genius can exist without a child inside him – this child is the source of all his energy! Because of the child within him, sometimes he can be a novice, sometimes he can be totally ignorant: he can touch realms about which he knows nothing. A mathematician who turns to poetry is never a loser. He comes back to his mathematics with a purer mind, with new experiences that are unknown to mathematics.

Nothing has ever been invented or discovered by someone who is strictly professional. It is always discovered by one who approaches the subject like an outsider coming with the mind of a child. Only a child is inventive, never an old man. The old man is an expert, and an expert cannot invent.

He will go on repeating the same thing, doing it and overdoing it; he will make it more perfect but never new. A professional cannot contribute constrictive and will focus on lack. Being connected to your intuition is expansive, connecting you with your deeper purpose.

It takes practice to begin shifting from your ego being the voice of command to your intuition being the guidance for direction. Approaching this from the Law of Attraction, you always want to go with the flow and be moving toward solutions instead of away from a problem. This reinforces the focus of turning a negative into a positive.

Neither perception is right or wrong; this is a personal choice. Based upon the Law of Attraction, whatever you focus on you will have more of in your life. You have to do what is best for you. People will try to influence your decision. The only person who can actually decide what is the best approach for you to take is YOU. This is your responsibility. It is your choice as to whether you want to be externally motivated or internally driven. Change is possible.

When everything lines up and there is congruency, you will be more likely to reach your goal. Determine which approach is best for you. What do you want more of in your life? You are the only one to determine whether your ego or intuition ought to be primary. Whatever goal you set for yourself, make sure that your thoughts, actions and words are aligned. When you have it all lined up, you are more likely to successfully reach your goals.

Understanding the Matrix of Self-Management

If you lack the iron and the fizz to take control of your own life, the gods will repay your weakness by having a grin or two at your expense. Should you fail to pilot your own ship, don't be surprised what inappropriate port you find yourself docked.

– Tom Robbins

The two key ingredients for making it all work are:

- Control
- Perspective

If you can maintain a sufficient level of each of these factors in yourself or in your organization, you probably won't find much room for improvement. Your world will be in order and you'll be focused exactly as you should be. Only when one or both of them slip away from optimal should you be concerned that something needs righting.

Control and perspective are closely intertwined dynamics, but achieving each one involves different approaches, whether the matter at hand is your teenager doing homework, your soccer team's practice, your next vacation, or your product launch. If your kitchen is a mess, for example, cleaning it up and placing all the tools and equipment where they belong will be a very different exercise from deciding what to cook and how to present it.

But the two activities remain very connected, in that without an organized kitchen, it will be very challenging to stay focused on the dinner itself; likewise, an insufficient focus on the recipes, the various components of the dinner event itself, and the plan for deploying them will allow the situation to quickly get out of control again.

A matrix constructed on the axes of control and perspective can be useful, both as a map for assessing your own standing with respect to these elements (or that of another person or a particular situation) and as a guide for improvement.

The four quadrants described by these axes identify, in very general terms, the syndromes that are typically experienced with the varying combinations of low and high control, and low and high perspective. The obvious optimal state would be elevated levels of both — the sector that is labelled "Captain and Commander."

Finding oneself in any of the other three quadrants, though, is not necessarily a bad thing. Just as any high-performance vehicle frequently gets off course, the best of us often fall away from the high-control, high-perspective state. It's the nature of human experience, which is always in some form of motion, to veer off course — sometimes in major, but consistently in minor, ways.

If, however, you tend to spend too much time in one of the less-than-optimal quadrants, you'll probably deserve the negative labels that are attached to them — Victim, Micromanager, or Crazy Maker. But these labels are best used as warnings for a course correction, much like the lane control bumps on a highway, when you drift as a result of your exploration and forward motion. In such cases a positive aspect will more aptly describe the syndromes — Responder, Implementer, and Visionary.

How individuals experience these quadrants of control and perspective are not cast in stone. You may, because of the nature of your temperament and personality, find yourself more frequently in one pattern than another. But you can easily move into a different quadrant depending on what you're doing and the level at which you are doing it.

For instance, you may have certain areas and projects under control, but not others. You may have a clear perspective on your finances but you're not sure where you're going in a relationship. Your desk is organized but your gym locker is a mess. Your personal life could be humming along nicely, but your professional situation could be in turmoil.

Your profile could also vary by horizon. You might have a clear set of goals for the following year and still have ambiguity about your job description. Your daily calendar and action lists could all be in order, and yet you might not be sure if the job you have is the right one for where you'd ultimately like to be in your career. You may be clear about your life purpose but uncertain about all the projects that you have commitments to complete in the near future. You could have a fulfilling set of personal affirmations and aspirations and still have three thousand unprocessed e-mails yelling at you in your inbox.

Not only can you be a Crazy Maker in your garden and a Micromanager in your golf game, but you can also move from one quadrant to another very quickly within one particular area of your life. You get on top of your workload and your job (Captain and Commander) and get so inspired that you wreak havoc by taking on a huge and ambiguous new project (Crazy Maker).

So you run around playing whack-a-mole to patch up the cracks (Micromanager) and then fall down exhausted, feeling like you've gone backward instead of forward (Victim). The next morning you get a grip (Responder), focus on where you're going again (Visionary), integrate your project's plan and actions into your total work inventory (Implementer), and take your partner to dinner because life is good and you're on track again (Captain and Commander).

So what? Our lives are full of an almost infinite number of situations and moments in which we could get more control or get a better viewpoint, or both. The first step in improving what's going on is acceptance of what is going on. If you try to resist or refuse to recognize current reality, you'll never find the handlebars. If you seriously try to make things work, it will be very useful to have an awareness of your own position in this matrix.

If you want to advance to the level of Captain and Commander, or ensure that you stay there, it is important to understand that there will be different strategies to adopt, depending on the situation in which you find yourself and your relationship to it. You may need more control, or more perspective, or both. And to achieve either of those, you may need to focus on different components of the prescriptive models. The secret to accomplishing all of this will be to notice what is most noticeable to you.

NOT ALL THAT GLITTERS IS GOLD

Making diversity initiatives work for you

It is important to keep our perspective when talking about the power of diversity to improve organisational performance. Diversity is powerful, yet is not a magical cure. On one hand, a diverse workgroup may be more creative and innovative. On the other hand, diversity can bring its own issues. So how can we keep diversity acting as a positive force for performance improvement?

Over the past decade, in most large corporations workforce diversity has become an important component of human resources management. This increasing attention is not only fashionable; it reflects important adjustments that globalisation and demographic changes demand.

Although diversity seems to be associated with some benefits on workgroup outcomes such as creativity and innovation, at the same time, workgroups that have a diverse composition often have problems such as communication breakdown and low cohesion. This is true when it comes to workgroups at any level. Some researchers have theorized that an equilibrium that avoids the two extremes of lowest and highest diversity is most likely to improve performance.

In general terms, we may describe the diversity problem as how to maintain and increase productivity when workgroups are increasingly diverse in their composition. In other words: how can we convert the weaknesses into strengths.

The diversity issue began as an effort to meet legal and governmental requirements. It has evolved to become a strategic priority aiming to improve a firm's position in the market. In fact, when firms explain why they operate diversity programs, they cite benefits such as becoming an employer of choice and attracting and retaining talent. Companies rarely cite legal or even ethical considerations. In other words, they see public and governments' diversity concerns as potential for business opportunity.

The visible and invisible diversity

The shift from a legal to a strategic view of diversity has also given the concept a new definition, where the 'legally protected' meaning – related primarily with race, gender, and age – has evolved into a more generic meaning that includes the entire spectrum of human differences.

Therefore, currently, diversity management refers to initiatives that involve both 'visible' and 'invisible' characteristics.

Among the 'visible' characteristics, we have: race, ethnicity, national origin, gender, age, and disability. Among the 'invisible' ones we may consider: mindscape (thinking style), hierarchical level, professional background, political and religious affiliation.

In his 1994 book, '*Mindscapes in Management*', the cybernetist Magoroh Maruyama stated back that the traditional management logic is the 'H' type, often associated with Americans. On the contrary, other countries are more the 'S' type...

Type H	Type S
Homogenising	Heterogenising
Hierarchical	Interactive
Classificatory	Pattern oriented
Competitive	Cooperative
Zero Sum	Positive sum
Sequential	Parallel

Clearly we will identify with some characteristics in each list – and probably the situation is more complex than we can portray in two lists. Nevertheless, we may find that any culture has an overall clear bias towards one of the profiles.

This difference is particularly obvious in the way a given culture understands time. We can relate monochronism with the H mindscape and polychronism with S. In other words, monochronic and polychronic time are only one aspect or dimension of the H and S mindscapes, which you may consider as the main patterns or types.

General Suggestions

We should not think that just having a diverse workforce will solve the firm's problems and automatically enhance the company's performance or improve its market position. That magical thinking is a myth.

To be effective, firms have to tailor their diversity initiatives to the situation, including the culture and unique business and people issues facing the firm. We will return to this point further ahead, at the globalisation section.

Another important point is that articulating up a culture that embraces diversity is an important component of an effective initiative. It is also important to clearly articulate how diversity supports the business strategy, particularly specifying how diversity contributes to the business objectives.

Effective conflict management is also crucial when managing diverse teams because the heterogeneous composition of a workgroup will trigger situations where opinions may collide.

In the following sections, I will discuss more suggestions related to diversity training and how American companies should manage diversity in their subsidiaries and affiliates.

Diversity Training

I suggest that training is the preferred method for managing diversity. Most of the time, firms provide such training programs – conducted either by in-house diversity staff or outside consultants – to both managerial and non-managerial employees. The training can promote awareness of discrimination and prejudice and improve behavioural skills of the employees in their interpersonal relations. The goal of diversity training is everyone working together effectively – and all with the goal of increasing the firm's success.

According to what we have seen, managers no longer view diversity training only as a socially responsible thing to do; they see diversity training as a strategic business decision that improve chances of being more competitive.

A survey in 1991 found that more than sixty percent of the firms questioned were conducting diversity training programs or were planning to do it. This number increased to sixty-six percent in 2001 and will probably reach over seventy percent during 2007.

Some research reports that white men are often reluctant to participate in a diversity training program. Perhaps that is because they are unlikely to believe it would bring any benefit or maybe because they fear it would be an occasion to blame them in some sense. On the contrary, women seem to believe that initiatives that help other groups will indirectly help to raise the awareness of their own discrimination issues, and therefore they are more prone to participate willingly in such programs.

One way of dealing with this white-male trainee reluctance is to start by introducing diversity concepts and make them accessible by using analogies and similes. For instance, one might describe diversity in terms of differences between professional orientations (such as production versus marketing), and then extend the concept to other 'invisible' domains – and then finally to the 'visible' ones.

The success of a diversity initiative depends a great deal on how we frame it. Within the past fifteen years, we have used the word diversity so frequently it is quite possible it has become loaded. People often seem to believe that the word is associated only with the 'visible' features.

Managers should frame diversity programs as challenges and opportunities rather than threats to overcome. For instance, names such as 'Cross-Cultural Awareness,' 'Working Together,' and 'Valuing Differences', seem to be more appropriate than those in which the word diversity actually appears in the title.

Diversity and Globalisation

Many firms with diversity management programs in their USA domestic operations are multinational corporations (MNCs) extensively involved in international markets and operating subsidiaries or affiliates in multiple nations. Although most of the USA MNCs have workforce diversity management programs in their domestic operations, the international diversity programs seem to be less well developed.

According to a journal article by Egan and Bendik (2003), many MNCs try to apply uniform policies and practices worldwide. In fact, even in countries with weak diversity regulation, administrative convenience and the equity of practices may motivate firms to voluntarily extend the coverage of their initiatives to overseas employees. Nevertheless, as we have seen, legal restrictions are not the only force promoting firms' increased attention to diversity. The wish to obtain, retain, and develop the workforce that will help the firm be competitive has led many employers to engage proactively in diversity efforts.

On the other hand, Human Resources is an area of corporate policy where global consistency is often difficult to implement. Furthermore, instead of 'cloning' US programs, diversity initiatives in Europe need to adapt to each employer's local needs and strategic objectives.

Europe has its unique diversity factors, such as the six million Roma people who the Economist (2001) described as a "spectral third world nation within Europe" and, potentially, "the most important civil rights issue in Europe."

The group's migratory tendencies might enforce this situation, especially due to the European Union principle of free movement of labour that will inevitably heighten the workplace management challenges of ethnic, national, linguistic, cultural, and religious diversity.

Another reason why we suggest a local treatment of diversity management is to avoid implications that diversity is an 'American management practice'. This prejudice can arise in other cultures, but it would be especially problematic if it is produced precisely here.

Business Ethics – A Practical Approach

Ethics and morality are viewed very differently by different people. Many believe that morality is something mandated by God or Gods. How do we determine what is right and wrong in general? One might think this is an easy question to answer. Others can see great complexity in the subject. Ethics are generally considered as being derived from morality.

So, what is morality? The generally taken definition for morality is 'being in accordance with the standards of conduct as determined by the society or system of ideas called into question'. Another definition would be 'that which is good for the person or society'. Most societies would agree that it is moral to give to the poor and it is immoral to steal from your neighbour.

As far as business ethics are concerned, how does one determine what is ethical and what is not? Many books have been written on the subject but who or what has the authority to dictate to us what is ethical and what is not? On what grounds are we to obey the 'ethical standard' and for that matter, what 'ethical standard' are we to adhere to?

This chapter presents a purely practical viewpoint on business ethics. First off, we will define business ethics as 'that which is best for the business in question'.

With this definition in mind, if it is 'best' for a business to steal or even commit murder then it is entirely ethical for the business to do so. That narrows the question down to 'what really is best for the business?'

Not too long ago I ran into a potential business partner. We agreed that he would provide a certain service (computer installation & networking) to a customer of mine on my behalf. I would bill my client and then pay him his portion of the bill (which was about 85% of the total). When he got to the client he convinced the client that they should deal with him directly and not pay me a 'cut' for doing nothing. He did the work for them, took the client from me and paid me nothing.

According to our definition was this ethical for him? He after all obtained a new client outright and ended up not having to pay anyone any part of the total profit.

Well, I provide training services to clients all the time. I always subcontract the work out to another company. What do you suppose the chances are that I will *ever* send this person to any of my clients again? In fact I have direct competitors who I am in continual contact with. We always share our resources.

That is, if my competitor-friend needs a network engineer and I know a good one, I refer him to them. What do you suppose the chances are that I will ever recommend this person to anyone. In fact I continually tell anyone looking for network engineers *not* to use this person because he has no 'business ethics'. I tell them that he will 'steal' their client.

The point is that the concept of business ethics is real, and is generally what we all think it is, but also that practically speaking, it really is 'that which is in the company's best interest'. That network engineer did successfully steal a client from me but he lost an awful lot of work, badly tainted his company's reputation in the market place and made a permanent business enemy in the process.

These days large businesses take business ethics *very* seriously. Understand that large corporations do *exclusively* what is in their best interest. Nevertheless, many of them are doing what will actually hurt their bottom line in the interest of adhering to strong business ethics.

Benevolence is defind as 'being kind to others'; giving 'selflessly'. If I give money to the poor they get money and I lose money. According to our definition above, you could construe that giving to the poor is an immoral act. But, when we give to the poor we accomplish many things for our society as a whole. Taxes can come down. More people in our society can become productive, thereby contributing to our overall well being rather than taking from it.

We personally feel a certain 'joy of giving' which lifts our morale and alleviates stress. We gain potential allies in both the people we help directly and others who see value in our benevolent acts. In general, by feeding the poor we help society as a whole. That makes our society a better place for us and our children to live.

If businesses spend large amounts of money on general education they lose money. However, the overall population becomes more educated. That means the companies find them easier to communicate with (advertise to) and the people they hire are better equipped to do their jobs. Problems that could devastate a society (and destroy business) are much less likely to occur because the people are better equipped to predict ensuing disaster and alleviate it.

The point is, a healthier, happier society in general is good for each member of that society. This principle goes for businesses as well as individuals. Bear in mind that business is created and operated exclusively for the benefit of individual people. That is, all business is made up of and for people.

If a business worked at polluting the World to a point where the World would *definitely* cease to sustain life within 5 years, that business would *definitely* cease to continue doing business (or dramatically change it) because the *people* running the business would not want to die.

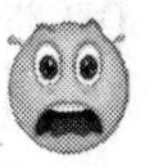

High-Stakes Decision Making: The Lessons of Mount Everest

Implications for leaders

On May 10, 1996, five mountaineers from two teams perished while climbing Mount Everest. Is there anything business leaders can learn from the tragedy?

This multi-lens analysis of the Everest case provides a framework for understanding, diagnosing, and preventing serious failures in many types of organizations. However, it also has important implications for how leaders can shape and direct the processes through which their organizations make and implement high-stakes decisions. The Everest analysis suggests that leaders must pay close attention to how they balance competing pressures in their organizations, and how their words and actions shape the perceptions and beliefs of organization members. In addition, the case provides insight regarding how firms approach learning from past failures.

Balancing competing forces

The Everest case suggests that leaders need to engage in a delicate balancing act with regard to nurturing confidence, dissent, and commitment within their organizations. First, executives must strike a balance between overconfidence on the one hand and insufficient confidence on the other. Leaders must act decisively when faced with challenges, and they must inspire others to do so as well. A lack of confidence can enhance anticipatory regret, or the apprehension that individuals often experience prior to making a decision.

High levels of anticipatory regret can lead to indecision and costly delays. This anxiety can be particularly problematic for executives in fast-moving industries. Successful management teams in turbulent industries develop certain practices to cope with this anxiety. For instance, some leaders develop the confidence to act decisively in the face of considerable ambiguity by seeking the advice of one or more "expert counselors," i.e. highly experienced executives who can serve as a confidante and a sounding board for various ideas.

Naturally, too much confidence can become dangerous as well, as the Everest case clearly demonstrates. To combat overconfidence, leaders must seek out information that disconfirms their existing views, and they should discourage subordinates from hiding bad news. Leaders also must take great care to separate facts from assumptions, and they must encourage everyone to test critical assumptions vigorously to root out overly optimistic projections.

Fostering constructive dissent poses another challenge for managers. As we see in the Everest case, insufficient debate among team members can diminish the extent to which plans and proposals undergo critical evaluation. Flawed ideas remain unchallenged, and creative alternatives are not generated. On the other hand, when leaders arrive at a final decision, they need everyone to accept the outcome and support its implementation.

They cannot allow continued dissension to disrupt the effort to turn that decision into action. As Cyrus the Great once said, leaders must balance the need for "diversity in counsel, unity in command." To accomplish this, leaders must insure that each participant has a fair and equal opportunity to voice their opinions during the decision process, and they must demonstrate that they have considered those views carefully and genuinely.

Moreover, they must clearly explain the rationale for their final decision, including why they chose to accept some input and advice while rejecting other suggestions. By doing so, leaders can encourage divergent thinking while building decision acceptance.

Finally, leaders must balance the need for strong buy-in against the danger of escalating commitment to a failing course of action over time. To implement effectively, managers must foster commitment by providing others with ample opportunities to participate in decision making, insuring that the process is fair and legitimate, and minimizing the level of interpersonal conflict that emerges during the deliberations.

Without strong buy-in, they risk numerous delays including efforts to re-open the decision process after implementation is underway. However, leaders must be aware of the dangers of over-commitment to a flawed course of action, particularly after employees have expended a great deal of time, money, and effort. The ability to "cut your losses" remains a difficult challenge as well as a hallmark of courageous leadership.

Simple awareness of the sunk cost trap will not prevent flawed decisions. Instead, leaders must be vigilant about asking tough questions such as: What would another executive do if he assumed my position today with no prior history in this organization? Leaders also need to question themselves and others repeatedly about why they wish to make additional investments in a particular initiative.

Managers should be extremely wary if they hear responses such as: "Well, we have put so much money into this already. We don't want to waste all of those resources." Finally, leaders can compare the benefits and costs of additional investments with several alternative uses of those resources. By encouraging the consideration of multiple options, leaders may help themselves and others recognize how over-commitment to an existing project may be preventing the organization from pursuing other promising opportunities.

Shaping perceptions and beliefs

The Everest case also demonstrates how leaders can shape the perceptions and beliefs of organization members, and thereby affect how these individuals will interact with one another and with their leaders in critical situations.

Hall and Fischer made a number of seemingly minor choices about how the teams were structured that had an enormous impact on people's perceptions of their roles, status, and relationships with other climbers.

Ultimately, these perceptions and beliefs constrained the way that people behaved when the groups encountered serious obstacles and dangers.

The ability to "cut your losses" remains a difficult challenge as well as a hallmark of courageous leadership.

– Michael A. Roberto

Leaders can shape the perceptions and beliefs of others in many ways. In some cases, the leaders' words or actions send a clear signal as to how they expect people to behave. For instance, Hall made it very clear that he did not wish to hear dissenting views while the expedition made the final push to the summit.

Most leaders understand the power of these very direct commands or directives. However, this case also demonstrates that leaders shape the perceptions and beliefs of others through subtle signals, actions, and symbols. For example, the compensation differential among the guides shaped people's beliefs about their relative status in the expedition.

It is hard to believe that the expedition leaders recognized that their compensation decisions would impact perceptions of status, and ultimately, the likelihood of constructive dissent within the expedition teams. Nevertheless, this relatively minor decision did send a strong signal to others in the organization.

The lesson for managers is that they must recognize the symbolic power of their actions and the strength of the signals they send when they make decisions about the formation and structure of work teams in their organizations.

Learning from failure

Often, when an organization suffers a terrible failure, others attempt to learn from the experience. Trying to avoid repeating the mistakes of the past seems like an admirable goal. Naturally, some observers attribute the poor performance of others to human error of one kind or another.

They blame the firm's leaders for making critical mistakes, at times even going so far as to accuse them of ignorance, negligence, or indifference. Attributing failures to the flawed decisions of others has certain benefits for outside observers. In particular, it can become a convenient argument for those who have a desire to embark on a similar endeavor.

By concluding that human error caused others to fail, ambitious and self-confident managers can convince themselves that they will learn from those mistakes and succeed where others did not.

The lesson for managers is that they must recognize the symbolic power of their actions and the strength of the signals they send.

– Michael A. Roberto

This research demonstrates a more holistic approach to learning from large-scale organizational failures. It suggests that we cannot think about individual, group, and organizational levels of analysis in isolation. Instead, we need to examine how cognitive, interpersonal, and systemic forces interact to affect organizational processes and performance. System complexity, team structure and beliefs, and cognitive limitations are not alternative explanations for failures, but rather complementary and mutually reinforcing concepts.

Business executives and other leaders typically recognize that equifinality characterizes many situations. In other words, most leaders understand that there are many ways to arrive at the same outcome. Nevertheless, we have a natural tendency to blame other people for failures, rather than attributing the poor performance to external and contextual factors.

We also tend to pit competing theories against one another in many cases, and try to argue that one explanation outperforms the others. The Everest case suggests that both of these approaches may lead to erroneous conclusions and reduce our capability to learn from experience. We need to recognize multiple factors that contribute to large-scale organizational failures, and to explore the linkages among the psychological and sociological forces involved at the individual, group, and organizational system level.

In sum, all leaders would be well-served to recall Anatoli Boukreev's closing thoughts about the Everest tragedy: "To cite a specific cause would be to promote an omniscience that only gods, drunks, politicians, and dramatic writers can claim."

Section III

Spirituality in Business, The right Way Out

Are You Ready to Evolve?

Life is change. Our lives ceaselessly change every second we live within it. When a species that walks this planet encounters a significant change species-wide, we call that change evolution. As human beings, we have gone through several such evolutions. Some of those changes were physical as we look at our progression from the men and women of "cave man" times. Other changes were mental, as we formed complex social structures, began to rely on agriculture and farming, our progression to the Industrial Age, and our solid hold on the Information Age. There are many people in the field of human potential and spiritual development that believe the next evolution will be a spiritual evolution. However, this evolution is different from all of the known previous evolutions that have taken place.

This cycle of evolution will focus more on the individual and that individual's ability to connect with spiritual energy. During this spiritual evolution, we will discover the oneness of all things.

We'll understand that the entity we call God is not a being, but rather an energy that exists within all things. We are a part of that spiritual energy and it is a part of us. All of our efforts in this next age, whatever it will be called, will be towards connecting to spiritual energy.

This evolution period consists of people choosing to analyze their current beliefs, exploring their true potential, becoming true individuals, and using meditation or meditative prayer as a way to connect to this infinite intelligence system. Peter Russell, author of "*Waking Up in Time*" describes connecting to the infinite spiritual energy through internal contemplation this way:

"The love of God. This is the love of which the great religions have spoken – the love of God. If God (and each of us has our own interpretation of that word) exists and loves us, it is not because of something we have done. God does not judge us as good or bad. Such judgments stem from our own needs, not God's. Nor does the love of God depend on how earnestly we worship God. That is merely another projection of our needs. The love of God is a love for our being, for the inner essence that dwells within us. This is the way we want others to love us. We want to be loved just as we are. Moreover, it is the way we would prefer to love others. To know the love of God is to have unconditional love in our own hearts. We want to be able to love in this way because inside we know that it is more lasting and more deeply satisfying than any conditional love."

Today, there are two species of human on the planet. You cannot differentiate these two species physically or by evaluation of mental capacity. One species of human believes they are a physical being. If you are a part of this species of human, you believe that you are your body, your beliefs, your cultural grouping, your socio-economic status, your race, your gender, your sexual orientation, your experiences, your memories, and your accomplishments. The other species of human believes they are one with God and that God is one with them. They believe that we are all interconnected and a part of the energy that pervades everything. This species believes that we are merely different expressions of the same energy, similar to how water can be expressed as gas, ice, mist, snow, rain, dew, salt water or fresh water. It's all water, but in distinctly different forms. As humans, we all have different forms, different languages, and different cultures, but we are all spiritual energy. We need merely to change our perception to recognize that fact.

The species of human that believes they are physical is the majority species on the planet today. When believing that we are our bodies, beliefs, or social classification, we create conflict. Our view that we are all different is solely responsible for every war ever fought over religion, property, human rights, or national power. It is because we believe we are different from one another that we then believe one must be superior to another. Slaves from Africa were only considered to be two-thirds human in the United States, which explains why it was easy for slave owners to treat the slaves so brutally. In American society, we see examples every day of people classified as rich gaining preferred treatment in the justice system, where someone less financially fortunate would not gain such leeway.

As we look at decades of fighting in the Middle East, we see a prime example of groups that believe themselves to be separate and distinct. Each group has caused pain and suffering for the other. Each group is responsible for taking over the other's personal property, for driving the other out of the land through force, for killing people of all ages and within both sexes, and for trying to get the world to side with their cause. The irony is that they fight over land, which is held in high esteem within Christianity, Judaism, and Islam – three of the largest religions in the world.

In the United States, we continue to deal with issues such as racial profiling, homophobia, selective hiring, exclusive neighborhoods, and a general intolerance for anything different from mainstream society. We have gotten better. We have come light years in terms of the expression of such hatred and negativity. However, lack of expression does not mean the energy of hatred and negativity has been eliminated. It is socially unacceptable to become violent for any reason these days. This is a step in the right direction, but the violence is a symptom of a deeper problem.

Society is eliminating a symptom, but the problems of separatist thinking lives on and is thriving.

The species of human that lives on the planet that believes they are a part of the energy of God and that energy is a part of them is a true minority, but is growing in numbers every day. If you are a part of this species, you believe that we are not separate beings, but different expressions of the same energy. In fact, not only would humans be a part of this energy, but literally all things. All animals, all trees, the chair you sit in, the computer you work on, the car you drive, and the clothes you wear are all a part of that all encompassing spiritual energy.

Those who want to connect to this energy consciously understand that they must be at peace to do so. In reaching spiritual energy, one must let go of thoughts and beliefs that prevent them from perceiving it. Imagine an onion. At the center of the onion is your soul. You must peel back all the layers of that onion before you reach the spiritual energy at its core. Each layer of the onion represents old beliefs or ways of being that continue to promote the thought that you are separate from everything else. As you peel back each layer, you are able to experience more and more of the higher consciousness. Your life begins to change as your thoughts about life change.

Peeling back all of the layers can be a life long pursuit. In fact, you may not fully experience the level of spiritual energy in this lifetime. However, just peeling back one layer will profoundly affect your life.

This evolution is a conscious one. It is an evolution that, for now, you can choose to participate in.

There is something known as "critical mass," which explains that when enough members of a species encounter the same change, the rest of the species will change with it. Therefore, it is entirely possible that at some point, if enough people choose the path of spiritual evolution, the entire human population could become one species again. A species that is reaching for its full potential, and full becoming what we know we can become...great!

Personal Peace

What image or thoughts does the idea of peace bring up for you? First thoughts of peace are of quiet, calm serenity. For most of us with our modern busy lifestyles it may well be a rare thing. A nice relax in the bath, a pleasant walk on an spring day or a day out somewhere with a friend all contribute towards giving you some peace.

Taking the concept of peace deeper makes us think of a time without strife, arguments or fighting. The ideal of people living together in harmony and showing respect and dignity towards each other also comes to mind. A life without worry can also be a life of peace.

Life does not give us the peace we want. External noise from traffic, people and machinery constantly invade on our attempts at quiet time. Demands from others stop us actually taking time out to relax. Wars and conflict at home and abroad all prevent peace being achieved. Concerns over how to pay the bills, personal health and those we love can also spoil our personal peace.

Are you at peace?

What is real 'personal peace' and how do you achieve it? As mentioned above a level of peace can be achieved by relaxing in pleasant surroundings

either on your own or with pleasant company. So can yoga, meditation, prayer or even just reading or doing a crossword puzzle. But how do you achieve a true inner peace?

To achieve real personal peace you need to be happy with yourself. Not other people, the state of the world or your home environment; just yourself. How can we be happy with ourselves? The answer is simple, rather dog-eared and cliched but true. We have to learn to love ourselves first, unconditionally. If you have children consider your love for them.

You want to do the best for them, keep them safe, help them grow. As they learned to walk you encouraged and praised them. They fell and hurt themselves, made mistakes. What did you do? Helped them up and on their way. You don't criticise a toddler for failing to walk by the time they reach their first birthday, or for falling over as they learn.

Neither should you beat yourself up over every mistake you make in life. Love yourself for who you are, what you were and what you will be to come. Be proud of your achievements, however small, because you worked for them. Don't criticise or be hard on yourself. Accept your mistakes, learn from them and move on.

Forgive yourself when you do wrong or let yourself or others down. If you can genuinely love and forgive yourself, and I mean 100%, warts and all, you are then on the way to being at peace with yourself. No amount of walking, yoga or meditation will give you peace if you don't love and forgive yourself as well.

Peace in a noisy world

So you are comfortable with who you are. You then switch on the tv or radio, open a newspaper and bang, there it all is, bad, bad news. Cynicism, fault finding and negative attitudes all creating an image of a terrible world full of terrible people.

Stop worrying about everything outside of your control. Learn to let go of things. Worrying nas never solved a problem but has contributed to personal ill health through poor diet and lack of sleep.

If it is not bad news that we are being bombarded with it is advertising that shouts at our subconscious mind telling us that buying things will bring us happiness. Neither the news nor advertising gives a balanced view of life. There are a lot of people out there doing good things as well as bad. Buying stuff does not always make us happy.

How to redress the balance?

The simplest thing to do is to avoid the bad stuff. If you want to keep your body healthy you eat a balanced diet, so to keep your mind healthy feed it a balanced diet! If you have a problem consider how you can solve it, rather than just worrying about it. If you cannot solve it learn to accept it or look for creative solutions. If you are still stuck let it go and see what happens.

Consider what you read and watch. Look for more upbeat material. Look around you and see the good stuff people do. Give yourself a new perspective on life and see how different everything looks!

It is all pretty obvious stuff but easier said than done. However by being aware and working at it you can make progress. It may be slow but it will be worth it. Relax and let it happen!

Spiritual Maturity – Growing Up, Wise!

Not for the feint of heart

Seekers of enlightenment fall into several categories, all of which, to the chagrin of those starting out on the path, are nearly mutually exclusive! As a person goes through life, their appetite for self-realization usually increases as they begin meeting influential personalities outside of their familiar (family) circle of close relatives and proximal neighbors.

At some point, parental influence is no longer as dominant as in the formative years, and a tripping point in beliefs is reached as the young seeker expands their field of vision beyond mere ego gratification (peer assistance) and business contacts (co-workers) defined by a particular social, industrial and/or religious structuring.

The family religion may be a help or a hindrance to those seeking the ultimate aim of life, which they may at first perceive as self-realization, then enlightenment, then spiritual guidance. If and when particular charismatic rituals and sanctified customs cease to appease the young soul, the seeker becomes vulnerable to the influence of charlatans, fakirs and wannabees who try to dazzle a new devotee with overwhelming waves of mystic sensation.

Induced escapism

The initiate may find themselves in all sorts of opulent, non-spiritual circumstances, including chemical (drugs), music (counter-culture) in a naïve attempt at material escapism. Although theoretically grounded, they are literally 'beside the wayside' and these activities mask themselves as cleverly disguised substitutes for authenticity. Upon further maturation, mostly derived from causal experience (trial and error) – the seeker will turn to time-honored, trusted sources of historical inspiration in various fields, such as mind development, philosophical thinking, reasoning, artistic expression, poetry, etc. In these avenues one will meet a bewildering assortment of more sincere, yet equally as discouraged as not fellow seekers who might seem to possess a common heritage.

Brotherhood of unity

What started as a personal quest for self-realization now becomes tinged with the possibility of cooperation and vested partnership of a much wider, spiritual community (of which there are many). Such a novice may at last be recognized as latent with potential, although still considered to be a spiritual adolescent.

Although the possibility of becoming pigeon-holed by dogma and intricate specialization is a definite reality at this stage and as much a trap as the previously mentioned forms of 'sincere escapism', it is a mark of religious piousness that can be ill afforded in a sectarian world.

Unity of purpose and commitment to the path are better than axle grease and ball bearings on the road to enlightenment. Spiritually mature individuals have a real head start in that they are able to distinguish and be recognized by genuine cosmic guides whose purpose is to assist the hungry souls who are moribund with the illusions of maya.

Purify and rinse

Expect hard change and loss of self-esteem that was placed too high on the scale during periods of pre-gestated vulnerability. Be willing to lose all that you had gained on the social, industrial, and religious scales of contrived artificiality. Be open to intense cleansing and absolute blind trust. Know that your path has been forged ahead and the way is clear, that there is a guide with experience to help open your heart and astral senses.

The spiritually mature is not certain to recognize their embryonic self of eons ago, indeed they are no longer the same person. One ego has been shed and its thin shell lies cast aside for the hungry vultures of the devil to devour. He can walk freely among formerly polarized points of distraction and attraction with a clear focus and open concentration.

The foot will not deviate into obstruction nearly as often, nor will adversaries attack a strengthened mind nor continue to fool a foolish heart. The mind is water-tight and iron clad with right purpose, the heart driven by an irresistible, otherworldly passion – and the foibles of man cease to intrigue.

The worthy opponent – your self

The one whom you thought is in your way is gone. The expansion of interconnected circles has brought you to a crossroads of selfish sorts. You emerge spiritually wiser and lighter with one less karmic influence to hold you back. Like a hot knife through butter your soul reeks of desire to join with your creator, and your creator has sent hand picked experts to challenge and nurture you. This should sound like a paradox because it is. No one said that enlightenment was easy. But now that you're here, would you go back?

Things I know for Sure

When I came into the world, I knew nothing, well, nothing that I could remember, that is. As you grow up, you learn many things, some you learn the hard way and others come in brief moments of blissful enlightenment. I like the later best. The older you get, the more you realize how little you know. When my kids make grandiose statements about life, I hold my little therapist mouth shut and think to myself, yeah, right, just wait.

For instance, I have never met anyone who is really bad. I know many people who are not yet enlightened, and others who are terrified to grow, but even the scariest of characters, who traipse into my office with a boatload of anger in tow, have tender hearts, wounded by terrible abuse.

The people who hurt themselves and others the most, have always been terribly hurt by someone else. I also know that when I can see the love inside a person, they begin to see it for themselves. I know that no matter how we'd like to avoid it, the ultimate responsibility for our reality and quality of life is ours. No excuses. Every choice has a consequence and every consequence either enhances or diminishes our life. It's not a New Age colloquialism, it's an in-your-face fact. Every good and bad thing in my life as an adult, I created. I own it, I can fix it, and I get to benefit from the lesson in it.

I know purity matters. The less you add to a Brightman or Bocelli voice, the more the beauty of it swells inside you. The less you add to a searing truth, the longer it vibrates through you. The less you speak and can sit in the silence, the more love you can feel from each other. The less you speak of how much you give, the more your character and soul evolve. Too much of anything, is still too much.

I know lies and distance kill relationships of every kind. I know cheating is never about the cheated upon. I know the misuse of power turns back on itself and destroys the abuser with untenable shame once he or she awakens. I know living deeply in the center of growth is the only meaningful way for one who is awake to thrive. I know that as Jack Kornfield says, after the ecstasy there will always be laundry.

I know that transformation does not mean you can't have unbridled lovemaking, peppermint ice cream, and laughter that brings you to tears. I know that we bump back and forth from being Buddha to butt-head with each changing thought and that too is spiritual. I know that we needn't fear death, because there is none. I know that we needn't fear life because our mistakes mean we are engaged and there are always second chances.

I know mean jokes, made up at another's expense are still mean jokes, even when people laugh. I know crude and vulgar are still crude and vulgar, no matter how you dress them up. I know that the strawberry I eat, comes to me from a calloused hands and the rights I have were born out of another's courageous heart. I know not to take anything for granted, not even my next breath.

I know that having a meeting with the pain, fear and evil inside, always makes them smaller and offers them a new, more comfortable role for both of us. I know as Pema Chodron says, "This body I am sitting in, right here, right now with all its aches and pains and pleasures, is exactly what I need to be fully human, fully awake and fully alive."

I know that when you can no longer help people heal, you plant in soil. When you can no longer hike tall mountains, you offer your hand to a child. I know that when you no longer read, you listen. When you can no longer hear, you feel. I know that when you can no longer do the things of your youth, you love, deeply, like crazy and that is the most important job you will ever have. I know integrity is all I take with me and I know love is all that matters, ever.

Your Belief Becomes Your Reality

Perhaps the most powerful single factor in your financial success is your beliefs about yourself and money.

The Determinant of Your Success

Perhaps the most powerful single factor in your financial success is your beliefs about yourself and money. We call this the Law of Belief. It says simply this: Whatever you believe, with feeling, becomes your reality. Whatever you intensely believe becomes your reality. That we have a tendency to block out any information coming in to us that is inconsistent with our reality.

What Successful People Believe

What we've discovered is that successful people absolutely believe that they have the ability to succeed. And they will not entertain, think about, or talk about the possibilities that they'll fail. They do not even consider the possibility of failure.

Positive Thinking Versus Positive Knowing

You always act in a matter consistent with your beliefs. The most important belief system you can build is a prosperity consciousness where you absolutely believe that you are going to achieve your financial goals. We call this positive knowing versus positive thinking. Positive thinking can sometimes be wishing or hoping. But positive knowing is when you absolutely know that no matter what, you will be successful.

The Foundation of Willpower

Another principle related to your beliefs is willpower. We know that willpower is essential to any success. Willpower is based on confidence. It's based on conviction. It's based on faith. It's based on your belief in your ability to triumph over all obstacles. And you can develop willpower by persistence, by working on your goals, by reading the biographies of successful people, by listening to audio programs, by reading books about people who've achieved success. The more information you take into your mind consistent with success, the more likely it is that you will develop the willpower to push you through the obstacles and difficulties you will experience.

Beat the Odds on Success

Remember that success is rare. Only one person in one hundred becomes wealthy in the course of a lifetime. Only five percent achieve financial independence. That means that the odds against you are 19-to-1. The only way that you're going to achieve your financial goals is if you get really serious. To succeed, you must get serious. You must get busy. You must get active. You must get going. Remember, everything counts.

Resolve to Achieve Greatly

Self-mastery, self-control, self-discipline are essential for anyone who wants to achieve greatly.

And control over your thoughts is the hardest exercise in self-mastery that you will ever engage in. See if you can talk and think about only what you desire and not talk or think about anything that you don't want for 24 hours. Then you'll see what you're really made of. It's a hard thing to do but with practice, you can reach the point where you are thinking about your goals and desires most of the time. Then, your whole life will change for the better.

Action Exercises

Here are two things you can do to build a belief system consistent with the financial success you desire: First, continually repeat to yourself the words, pictures and thoughts consistent with your dreams and goals. Whatever you repeat often enough, over and over, becomes a new belief. Second, set a goal for yourself to think and talk only about the things that you want for the next 24 hours. This will be one of the hardest things you ever do. But if you can keep your mind on what you want and off of what you don't want for 24 hours, you can begin to change your entire future.

Give in Without Giving Up

What do you do when it feels like there is no light at the end of the tunnel? When everything is in doubt and life's possibilities seem empty? When you watch world events transpire over which you have no control and film and music idols, once seemingly immortal, senselessly succumb to cancer or drugs?

The economy is uncertain. The future of your environment is uncertain. The future of your health is uncertain. The more dismal you feel, the more you panic. As you panic, the more prone you are to illness in body and mind. The cycle accelerates and intensifies until you feel helpless and hopeless.

What do you do when you feel stuck between living in fear or not living at all? I recently had this very conversation with my taxi driver in Turkey. For some reason, we started talking about the most beautiful places to go in the country.

And while he mentioned a few places that he loved most, he also said that he could no longer enjoy these places because he was unable to take pleasure in anything. He complained that he felt trapped in a dark place and was unsure if he would ever get out.

He had lost his job over two years ago, followed by his house, two cars and wife of 20 years. He drove a taxi out of necessity, not out of choice. It paid the bills, just barely. The war had taken the life of his son. His new girlfriend was just diagnosed with breast cancer. He feared he would lose her too. He used to write. Now, he could not find words. He used to sing. Now, he could not find his voice. He prayed every day for god to help, but no help had come. He tried to "think positive", but only negative thoughts appeared.

"I don't know what to do anymore," he said, before apologizing for throwing his problems my way. "How can I keep going if I don't know that everything will eventually turn out well?"

"We cannot control the future," I said. "I am not a fortune-teller and I cannot know what any specific outcome will be. I can know, however, that if you panic or feel hopeless, it is not going to help anything, but rather make the situation worse."

I told him that he had every right to feel panicked and depressed. The truth is, I explained, that it was physiologically impossible to think positively when he was deep in stress and fear. Hormones and the other biochemical changes in the mind and body were keeping him from being able to do so. It is as if he was trying to stop shivering when feeling cold. "You cannot access good behaviours and positive emotions when you are deep in the fear response. It is like trying to drive your car without any gas," I explained.

"The solution is to surrender," I told him.

"Give up and die?" he asked.

"No," I answered. "Give in and live."

I continued by explaining that 'surrender' meant to stop fighting or struggling and allow himself to simply receive, like a fetus does in the mother's womb. He had to allow himself to imagine that he was receiving all the magic, power and support that the universe has to offer, filling him up, so that he could then find the strength and courage to face life.

I told him to imagine an image of a mother made of light, with her wings spreadwide, holding him like an infant, rocking and cradling him, while saying these words:

"You are loved. You are valued. The support you need is here." He should say this over and over, for as long as he wished.

I instructed him to do this exercise after he prayed and any other time he felt fear, panic or negativity rising up. If he did, he might find that as he changed on the inside, his life or at least the way he acted in his life, would change in a positive way too.

By doing this exercise enough times, I explained, his unconscious mind might take in the experience as real. In effect, he would essentially be reprogramming old beliefs of scarcity, of not being enough, or having enough of all that he needs. As his beliefs change, attitudes, behaviours and interactions with others change. Rather than being shut down and shut out, he could be open to his own abilities and the resources others could offer. The possibilities become endless rather than pointless.

"Will I get my old job back?" he asked.

"I can't tell you that," I answered. "You might find yourself doing something else entirely. Whatever it is though," I added, "you may find yourself content and able to appreciate and take pleasure again. You will find your words and perhaps your voice will discover a beautiful melody. It is through our suffering and the depths of despair that we uncover greatness."

"Did you ask for help this evening? I mean, why is it do you think, that we are having this conversation?" I asked. "yes," he answered, "I did."

"Well then," I continued. "I offer you a wish that all the love and support the universe has to offer find their way to you."

A little gleam came into his eye – perhaps a tear or perhaps a shred of hope – and with a smile on his face he said, "Today I will go to the synagogue and pray for you too. I will pray that you also receive all the support and love you need to continue on your path; to inspire others like me to remember that we are ultimately loved, not punished."

I never got his name, but in that moment in time, his heart opened. Mine did too. In these difficult times, all we can do is to surrender, give in, and open our hearts to one another, to receive and give. Love is the source of our survival.

It's About the Climb

We live in a fast paced world; fast cars, fast food, jet planes, cell phones, laptops etc. All of these technical and life style changes have had a definite impact on society, both positive and negative. On the positive side, we have become the richest, most comfortable and most fortunate nation in the world. Our day-to-day lives surrounds us with conveniences future generations never experienced and present generations across the globe strive to emulate.

On the negative side it has made us the most greedy, materialistic and entitled generation to ever inhabit the earth. Each of our days are full of the desire for more of everything; more money, bigger houses, more toys, more vacations etc.

Having the desire and wishing for a better life is not the issue. God want's all of his children to attain the finer things in life, not struggle. It's when we are blessed with enough and are not aware of the others that touch our lives. It's when we take them for granted, forget to be thankful and grateful or refuse to share with those less fortunate that it damages our soul and sense of being.

We focus so fervently on attaining, that we forget to give back and nurture life and ourselves. We've become so obsessed with obtaining more of everything, we are often not living in the present but acquiring for the future. What this means is that we spend so much of out time looking ahead, that we forget were we are. When our life consists of taking from what life has to offer and not giving back, it's only a matter of time before the well runs dry.

Don't get me wrong, we all need to plan to improve our lives, protect our families and make our lives more secure if we can. But at what price? Certainly not at the expense of our own good will and the consideration for our fellow man and planet.

It's not always about more, how fast you can get there or what's on the other side. When you're so focused on more i.e. bigger, better, faster, I promise you that you'll lose contact with yourself and what really matters in life, the present.

The true joys of life, the simple things are free; a hug, a smile, a walk by the ocean, the scent of a flower, the song of a bird, catching a sunrise or sunset. These are the wonderful aspects of life that you are trading and losing, if you are constantly focused on more.

When is enough, enough? When you lose your sense of self, a loved one whom you've ignored or realize your child is graduating from high school or college and you hardly know them.

Today is all you have, today and all the wonderful and beautiful pieces of your life that are part of that day. Life is not about how fast you can get from point A to point B, it's about the journey. The journey is where everything that your heart and soul require lives; joy, love, hope, faith, courage, adventure, wonder, friendship and making a difference in someone's life.

Likewise, life is not about what's on the other side of the mountain, is about what's here today, it's about the climb. Who's in your day today, which loved one or friend are you with or should you be with? Who's climbing the mountain with you, eager to be by your side, to hear your voice, see your smile, hold your hand? Wake up and get present. Enjoy the climb today for someday when, the climb will end. God wants us all to be healthy and happy but not at the expense of ignoring ourselves, our loved ones and our fellow man. You can't give to someone else, what you can't give to yourself. More does not nourish the soul or the spirit, it feeds the ego. If you would begin to slow down and focus on what you're feeling versus what you're thinking, you'll begin to reconnect with your heart and soul. Only then will you begin to enjoy the climb and be grateful for those in your life.

Section IV

Towards Self-Awareness and Enlightenment

- Spiritual Intelligence: The Intelligence of Today
- Seven ways to develop or raise spiritual intelligence
- Creating The New You
- Creating The Life You Really Want
- From Complaints To Commitments
- Manage Your Energy

Spiritual Intelligence: The Intelligence Of Today

A Chinese proverb says, *"When the pupil is ready, the teacher will come."*

More and more people everywhere are becoming ready and concerned with the untapped potential of the mind and consciousness. Previously, particularly in education circles, if you talked about inner voices, outer signs, or a guiding presence, you would be discounted or put away; today being committed is fine. The materialism and individualism of Western culture have created an empty space in the lives of a lot of people and there is a growing need for spirituality; a search for community as a result of urbanization; and a search for identity in an increasingly depersonalized society. People have become more and more disenchanted with experts in every field; and they are beginning to trust their own inner authority to seek a purposeful path, to create their own vision, and to realize a sense of empowerment.

Spiritual Intelligence Is Deep Self-awareness

Humans are essentially spiritual beings, evolved to ask fundamental questions. "Who am I?" "Where am I going?" "What do others mean to me?" It is an ability to answer questions like these that lead people to personal growth workshops. Spiritual intelligence motivates people to balance their work schedules to spend time with the family. Or an executive with a high SQ might look beyond profit margins and devote time for voluntary work with orphans. Spiritual intelligence also addresses the need to place one's life in a shared context of value.

The transformative power of SQ distinguishes it from IQ and EQ. IQ primarily solves logical problems. EQ allows us to judge the situation we are in and behave appropriately. SQ allows us to ask if we want to be in that situation in the first place. It might motivate us to create a new one. SQ has little connection to formal religion. Atheists and humanists may have high SQ while someone actively religious may not.

Spiritual intelligence can be described as a deep self-awareness in which one becomes more and more aware of the dimensions of self, not simply as a body, but as a mind-body and spirit. When we employ our spiritual intelligence, we reach the extraordinary place in which our mind no longer produces data of the type wanted or needed and the need for intuition becomes accelerated. As conscious beings, we are aware of our thought images and feelings as they arise in our consciousness; yet our complex and not so complex processing of information in the brain leads to an inner experience. This inner experience represents the essence of spiritual intelligence. As we find our inner voices, the whisperings of supra consciousness and go within, we find our spiritual connection. By accessing these inner processes, we can learn to nurture and develop our spiritual intelligence.

What Spiritual Intelligence Is And What Spiritual Intelligence Is Not

Inner Knowing

Spiritual intelligence enables us to develop an inner knowing. In the language of Indian philosophy, inner knowing is to know the essence of consciousness and to realize that this inner essence is the essence of all creation. Spiritual intelligence provides us access to higher consciousness in which there is an awareness of rapport, an awareness of being one with the universe, and all its creatures, of a knowing, a "gnosis."

Deep Intuition

Spiritual intelligence connects us with the Universal mind or Big Mind and problem solutions that come from deep intuition are to the benefit of all, not one solution at the expense of others. Through the use of spiritual intelligence, we can become integrated, if we are willing to turn over choice to the authentic conscience or to deep intuition. (Jung, 1969)

Oneness with Nature and the Universe

Spiritual intelligence enables us to become one with nature and to be in harmony with life processes. Spiritual intelligence urges us to search for wholeness, a sense of community and a sense of relationship, to create an identity and to search for meaning; and out of this search for meaning will come a sense of empowerment.

Problem Solving

Spiritual intelligence enables us to see the big picture, to synthesize our actions in relation to a greater context, which then in turn becomes "life meaning." (Frankl, 1985). With spiritual intelligence we can identify and solve problems of meaning and value; to offer solutions directed toward the benefit of all. Spiritual intelligence is not amoral, it engages us in questions of good and evil and affords us opportunities to dream, to reconfigure, and to look beyond the boundaries of a situation to what it could be.

Core experiences of spiritual intelligence

An awareness of ultimate values and their meaning, peak experiences, a feeling of transcendence and heightened awareness are all part of spiritual intelligence core experiences in action. These core experiences may by their nature seem fleeting; however, if they are intrinsic to human nature as psychologists Abraham Maslow (1971) suggested more than three decades ago in *The Farther Reaches of Human Nature*, the question becomes one of how to study, nurture and develop spiritual intelligence.

Nurturing and developing spiritual intelligence

One of the primary aspects of nurturing spiritual intelligence is to bring one's life into perspective. What does this mean for the individual? You can bring your life into perspective by reflecting upon your values, perhaps by asking the big question that Carl Jung loved to pose to his friends and colleagues: 'What myth are you living?' To develop spiritual intelligence, we need to take time to see a vision of our lives, identify the goals and desires that we have and to create a balance in our lives. You can ask yourself questions in a meditative quiet state, and remember that it is important to believe that you will receive the answers.

Educating for spiritual development and higher consciousness has within it the hope and goal of developing the student's ability to use their spiritual intelligence to discover what is essential in life, particularly in their own lives, and to recognize what they can do to nourish the world. Defining spiritual intelligence as the ability to access one's inner knowledge, likely traits of spiritual intelligence are listed below, as well as suggestions on how to strengthen these traits for learning.

LIKELY TRAITS	HOW TO STRENGTHEN FOR LEARNING
Uses inner knowing	Provide time for reflective thinking
Seeks to understand self	Use journal writing and processing
Uses metaphor and parables to communicate	Read lives / works of Spiritual Pathfinders
Uses intuition	Use problem solving (predicting)
Sensitive to social problems	Conduct service learning projects
Sensitive to their purpose in life	Use personal growth activities
Concerned about inequity and injustice	Use problem-based learning
Enjoys big questions	Provide time for open-ended discussion
Sense of Gestalt (the big picture)	Use mapping and thematic studies
Wants to make a difference	Develop personal growth activities
Capacity to care	Study lives of Spiritual Pathfinders
Curiosity about how the world works/functions	Integrate science / social sciences
Values love, compassion, concern for others	Use affirmations / think-about-thinking
Close to nature	Employ eco-environmental research
Uses visualization and mental imagery	Read stories and myths

Reflective, self-observing and self-aware	Use role playing / sociodrama
Seeks balance in life	Discussion/goal setting activities
Concerned about right conduct	Employ process discussions
Seeks to understand self	Trust intuition and inner voice
Connected with others, the earth and the universe	Stress unity in studies
Peacemaker	Use what, so what, now what model
Concerned with human suffering	Study lives of eminent people

SEVEN WAYS TO DEVELOP OR RAISE SPIRITUAL INTELLIGENCE

To develop or raise spiritual intelligence, there are a number of methods that can be employed; these include an emphasis on the core values of community, connectedness and oneness of all, compassion, a sense of balance, responsibility and service. These core values call for the use of a multisensory approach to problem solving and life; relying not only on the five senses, but including visualization, meditation and deep intuition. Given this premise, there are essentially seven ways to raise or develop spiritual intelligence.

They include:

1. Think about your goals, desires and wants to bring your life into perspective and balance, and identify your values.
2. Access your inner processes and use visualization to see your goals, desires and wants fulfilled; and experience the emotion connected with this fulfillment.
3. Integrate your personal and universal vision and recognize your connectedness to others, to nature, to the world and to the universe.
4. Take responsibility for your goals, desires and wants.
5. Develop a sense of community by letting more people into your life.
6. Focus on love and compassion.
7. When chance knocks at your door, let it in and take advantage of coincidences.

Inherent in these seven ways to develop your spiritual intelligence is engaging in finding a sense of purpose and creating a vision. Once your vision is created, then there must be a commitment to it, followed by the intention or will to carry through toward your identified goal, desire or want. Essential to the development of your spiritual intelligence is sensing the connectedness of everything to everything, and shifting one's focus of authority and perception in life from external to internal.

Equally essential to the development of spiritual intelligence is the recognition of your relationship to the earth. The importance of earth-centered reverence and connectedness was drawn from Ancient Wisdom and Eastern Mysticism. Among many Native American traditions, and in the Hermetic, Sufi, Zen, Tao and Confucianism traditions, there is a clear emphasis on caring for the earth and being in harmony with nature.

In the seven ways to nurture and develop spiritual intelligence, we suggest infusing your goals, wants and desires with emotion; and this premise is based on the finding that access to unconscious processes is facilitated by attention to feelings, emotion, and inner imagery as suggested by Ancient Wisdom and Eastern Mysticism. Spiritual intelligence is not limited in the ordinary ways that we might expect the mind to be limited, since access to one's spiritual intelligence through the use of inner knowing can be facilitated to an extent that is ultimately unlimited. In the words of Arnold Toynbee:

The ultimate work of civilization is the unfolding of ever-deeper spiritual understanding.

Creating the New You

"Reinvention" implies a process of deconstruction, a subsequent reconstruction, and a resultant new thing. Reinventing yourself ideally results from a candid examination of your life and a determination to improve it by taking positive action leading to your new goals whether a better job, happier work-life balance, or a healthier lifestyle. Changing yourself superficially as a reaction to circumstances, such as undergoing plastic surgery or buying new clothes and a flashy car, will not get to the root dissatisfactions in your life.

Cheryl Simpson believes that there are five key steps to a true personal reinvention: taking an honest inventory of who you are, clarifying your values, identifying your aspirations and passions, brainstorming prospects, and marketing yourself successfully. If you feel that it's time for you to begin your life anew, keep in mind that others have done the same thing, successfully, and that you need to keep your focus on how to reinvent yourself so that it's neither cosmetic nor temporary.

What You Need to Know

I feel stuck in my current job, and although I like the company I work for I'm not sure that this is the career path for me. What can I do?

Changing jobs can be a terrific way to begin a major personal transition. Before you decide where you should be working, do a thorough audit of what it is you are seeking in your career. First of all, think about jobs you would like to do and whether you have the skills to undertake them. If you aren't sure what a different job entails, ask if you can speak to someone in that field to get insight into that position and career.

Use printed and online resources to find out additional information. If more training or experience will be needed to enter that field, talk to the human resources department to find out if your company offers that training or where it is available. Broach the subject in a positive way with your line manager, focusing on your desire to improve rather than on feeling stuck.

I would like to change my career direction, but my résumé reflects who I was, not what I want to become. How can I convince prospective employers to give me an opportunity?

A wealth of advice is available in books and online about writing a résumé. These sources will give you insight into identifying transferable work skills and activities in your personal life that are relevant to your desired role. Do some research and draft a new résumé based on what you've learned. Ask a good friend for his or her reaction to the new document.

Don't be afraid to share your passions and aspirations with your prospective employers this will help them see past any omissions in your previous experience. Remember that passion for a role is very attractive to recruiters; just think about how many uninspiring (and uninspired!) applications they have to sift through every day.

I've found that my values aren't those of my employer, and I'm feeling increasingly uncomfortable in my job. Is it worth staying on?

Values are strong personal beliefs that aren't up for negotiation. You may be able to appear to take on values that aren't your own, but, under pressure, your values will reassert themselves. You will be a misfit in the company and uncomfortable with yourself. It's much better to look elsewhere for a new job where your values are shared.

What to Do

Take Stock: For many people, the planned career path takes unplanned twists and turns. One often hears people describe how they decided what they wanted when they left school, followed the recommended route to get there, and now are dissatisfied at what they've ended up doing.

The pressures of modern life drive us toward making choices that bring an illusion of security, status, and success. We find a good job and are sucked into the promotional slipstream while being paid an increasingly large salary as we advance in the company. At the same time, the accompanying benefits, such as health care and company pension plans, make us reluctant to change our lives radically.

Once we realize we're unhappy, we try to rationalize our way out of it, convincing ourselves that we've invested too much in our employing organization and our careers to risk starting again at the beginning. So we struggle on, perhaps resentfully, fantasizing about how it could have been. Sometimes, we're fortunate enough to be assisted in overcoming our resistance to change. We're laid off, we suffer ill health, our family circumstances change, a significant relationship comes to an end, and so on. This external trigger often results in personal reinvention and is often perceived to be a blessing in the long run.

The challenge for most people is to arrive at the decision to make adjustments in their lives before such a dramatic catalyst intervenes. Being able to sense the imbalance in your life, the drawbacks of your current job, and the gulf between who you are and who you would like to be is key to making meaningful personal changes. Once you decide to reinvent yourself, it's important to keep in mind, as Jane Herman says, that it's an "inside job": "reinvention is an inside job meaning that it is the changes we make on the inside that create the most powerful and long-lasting differences in our lives."

Below is a series of steps that may help you through the reinvention process.

Carry out a Personal Audit

Assess your life from a personal and professional perspective. Write your name in the center of a blank sheet of paper, and itemize your life's pressures and disappointments on the left and the pleasures and delights on the right. Write down everything you think is relevant, including the interests and aspirations that you had early in your career and all the things that have given you happiness since then.

Highlight the "break points" on both sides of the analysis so that you can easily identify issues that really need to be addressed. The intention here is to find a way of swinging the balance of your life toward the pleasurable side of the diagram by drawing out the elements of your life that characterize you and your preferred role.

Think about Your Ideal Scenario

Think about what you'd do if you were free from practical or financial limitations and write everything down at the top of your sheet of paper. This is a freeing exercise that may put you in touch with what it is you would prefer to be doing. Don't censor your ideas or cast them aside on the basis that you don't have enough money or security to achieve them.

Identify Obstacles

At the bottom of the page, write down things that are preventing you from the full enjoyment of your professional and personal life. These are the barriers that you must overcome in order to achieve a satisfactory reinvention. They usually manifest as fears, for example: 'I will lose my pension/benefits/financial security,' 'I have dependents and can't risk letting them down,' 'I have major financial commitments and won't be able to meet these if I change my job,' or 'I can't afford to start something from the beginning at this stage of my career'.

You hold each of these fears without question. So question them. Are they really true? Do they really matter? If you allow your life to be governed by your fears, how will you feel at the end of your career? Is this acceptable to you?

Make Changes\and Live Them

Now that you've done the thinking, you can start making changes. Working through the process above has allowed you to see your life objectively and should help you pinpoint areas that need the most attention. If you have a strong feeling about the need to change something, don't try to reason your way out of it: follow your instincts and see what happens. If you curb your impulses by rationalizing them, you'll end up behaving same way time and time again.

To others, and indeed to yourself on some levels, your actions may not seem reasonable, but many people have benefited from taking a risk at points in their life. 'Act first and reflect later' has probably been the pattern of your career to date, so try something new, see if it works, then adopt or discard your initiative as appropriate.

Deciding to change, but not acting on your decision, will not alter your situation. Even if the changes seem alien to you to begin with, practice them until they feel normal. Once you start behaving like the person you want to be, people will start treating you as if you are that person. You cannot change your life without changing your behaviour patterns.

You'll see that reinvention isn't really what's going on here. The effect is reinvention; the fact is that you're bringing to the surface a latent part of your character that seeks full and happy expression. Make the decision to live the way you want to fully and without apology.

What to Avoid

You Rush Your Reinvention: Some people decide to make radical changes in their lives and jump into a reinvention without thinking through what is actually required. This only leads to disappointment. Enthusiasm is vital for any attempt at personal change, but it needs to be balanced with considered decisions and a deep understanding of yourself.

Without these, you'll make changes that don't last and end up feeling disillusioned and de-energized. Work through the process above and ask a trusted friend to help you if you feel you're not making progress.

You Give Up: Changing behaviors takes time, and it's common to backslide into your old ways. Focus on the positive actions you are taking, not your failures. Determine each day to do the best you can, and remind yourself throughout the day how your new behaviors will help you reach your goals.

Creating the Life You Really Want

We may not have control over what happens to us, but we do have control over what we do about it and our reactions to it. The response we have to any given situation is up to us, it is our choice, and every choice we make has led us to the place we are today.

This is not a bad thing, if we could have done better we would have. The good news is since we have created our lives to be the way they are, we also have the power to create them to be exactly the way we want them to be. I believe that there are three basic things we can do right now to start changing and creating our life to be the way we want it to be. Those three things are:

Know That The Present Is Perfect

Get rid of all the tolerations in our lives and get complete with the past, practice extreme self care.

The Present Is Perfect

Prasad is an old friend of mine. He has become one of the greatest teachers in my life. Prasad is a great example of living in the present, and making the present perfect. Prasad simply eats when he is hungry, drinks when he is thirsty and takes a nap in the afternoon, if that feels right. If he cannot get someone to play with him, he finds a favourite toy and entertains himself.

For Prasad, the present is perfect. Many of us are driven by our need to resolve the past or to create a perfect future. There isn't anything wrong with either approach, but they do have one weakness. The weakness is that neither is about the present moment, both are about a different time than now. There are times when it is valuable to clear up the past, and there are times when it is valuable to visualize the future, but only if done with both feet firmly planted in the present.

What is the present? The present is simply today. What is happening this moment. It is what is now, not yesterday, or what could be tomorrow, but right this very moment. There is a richness in the present, and a power that enables us to create wonderful things. When we are able to stay present to the moment, to be with it and in it, magical things happen. By staying in the present we are able to put the past and the future into perspective.

Accepting that the present in perfect doesn't mean we have to be satisfied or happy with it. It just means that we accept that things are the way they are for a reason and that we have a choice in this very moment, we can either do nothing about it or change it.

My best friend Nancy always tells me, "either do something about it or quit complaining about it." Each moment is a new opportunity to begin creating our lives to be the way we want them to be.

I believe this concept especially applies to our weight and how we feel about ourselves. Once I asked my spouse if I looked fat in something, whose reply was "what are you going to do about, loose ten pounds in the next ten minutes." The fact is I could not do anything about it except be happy with the way I was and make a choice to make some changes if I want to lose the ten pounds. I think the key to successful weight loose and maintenance is to accept ourselves the way we are and love ourselves for who we are, not for our dress size.

The first step in living in the present is to take a look at your life and see how much time you are living in the present. If it is less than 90%, you are missing out on the richness of the moment. A very good friend of mine use to say "Every day above ground is a good one." Each moment is a gift, a precious gift that we can give to ourselves.

An affirmation that keeps me grounded and centered and reminds me that the present is perfect is, "this is the best day of my life." It reminds me that this is the only day of my life, the past is gone and the future is not promised. Live every day as if it were your last, as if this moment were all that you had left. Make each moment count.

Tolerations

Tolerations are those little things in your life that suck your energy. They do not have to be major, in fact it is usually the little things in life that get to us. It can be a leaky faucet, a loose wheel, or those ten extra pounds. Tolerations can also be major, like an abusive co-worker, a major car problem or over extended credit cards. Whatever the toleration, it takes our energy and does not allow us to be totally present in the moment.

Most people think that they are not tolerating anything, or at least not very much. I was the same way when I first heard about the concept. It was all I could do to come up with five tolerations. Then I really started thinking about it and ended up with 146!

One of my tolerations has always been my weight. Even when I weighed 128 pounds, at 5 feet 7 inches that is thin, it was not thin enough. I thought if I could only loose five more pounds I would be perfect. After taking a serious look at my weight I realized that what I was really tolerating was a low self-esteem and a societal message that thin equalled beauty and self worth.

It was only after I accepted that I was never going to be model thin, I was not willing to work that hard, did I come to peace with myself and change my attitude from one of tolerating my weight to appreciating who I am. I changed my focus from my weight to establishing healthily habits, eating more fruits and vegetables, drinking water and exercising. I also no longer tolerate anyone saying anything about my weight, including myself.

The truth about tolerations is that they can:

Hold Us Back

Cause Grief

Waste Time

Take Continuous Energy

Make Us Less Conscious

Take Away From Our Integrity

Take Us Off Purpose

Make Us Feel Bad About Ourselves

Keep Us From Totally Being Present

Getting rid of tolerations frees us up to be more in the present with fewer distractions.

We cannot know what we do not know. Once we become aware of all the things we are tolerating, we can then do something about it. Make a list of 10 things you are tolerating in your life and commit to having those things cleaned up within one week. Once those are completed, list ten more, and continue to work on your tolerations until you no longer are tolerating anything. By doing this one thing, you will create more space and energy in your life, and be freer to create the life you really want.

Get Yourself Complete

Tolerations have a sister, they are called completions. Tolerations deal more with things, completions deal with people or experiences. Tolerations usually are outside of us. Incompletions are more about what is going on inside of us. Incompletions are those things in our past that we have not let go of or forgiven. Much like tolerations, they nag at us and take our energy. They are like background noise, constantly humming away, distracting us from totally being in the present.

In addition to the incompletion being on our mind, we might experience other emotions that remind us of the incompletion such as pangs of guilt, remorse, or regret. There may be shame related to the incompletion, or anger. Denial can accompany an incompletion, or sadness. Being incomplete means being unresolved, the experience or relationship might be over, but not yet complete.

How do we know if we need to get complete with someone or something in our lives? If there is anyone in our life that we would feel uneasy about bumping into or there is an experience that we just as soon avoid thinking or talking about, there is probably something we are not complete with in that relationship or situation. How do we get complete?

Some suggestions I would make are: if you borrowed it return it, if you loaned it out and want it back ask for it or write it off if the item is never going to be returned. If you have hurt someone, apologize, even if it means calling someone you have not talked to in fifteen years. And if someone has hurt you, forgive them. This does not make them right, it simply frees you and allows you to move on with your life. This one might take a while, but it will be well worth the effort.

Getting complete will create more opportunities for you by opening up space in your life. You will have more confidence because you will know that you have done the best possible job of cleaning up your past. You will have more time because you will be focused in the present and not drug down by the past and you will have fewer problems.

When going through this process the first thing I had to do was return my over due library books and pay the fine of $50.00. Not a fun thing to do but it got it off my mind, I felt great that I had kept my commitment, since borrowing means just that, and I learned a valuable lesson, it is cheaper to keep agreements than to let them get over due. Get complete, you will feel better.

Extreme Self Care

The final part of this equation is extreme self care. One might think that extreme self care sounds selfish, and besides who has time to take care of themselves. Most people are busy taking care of family, friends, the boss..... In reality, taking good care of yourself helps you take care of everyone else in your life, better. By making sure you are healthy, well rested and pampered, you are able to give more to the people in your life, you will have more energy and more zest for life.

When I think of taking care of myself first, I am reminded of travelling on an airplane. During the safety procedure, the flight attendant always instructs the passengers that in case of an emergency, the oxygen bag will drop down from the compartment above our heads. We are told to take the oxygen mask and put it over our mouth and nose, then any small children or others that need assistant.

We are instructed to always put our own mask on first. Why do we do that? Because if we take care of everyone else first, we might not have the oxygen we need to take care of ourselves. If we do not take care of ourselves first, we might not be able to later. One of the best ways to start taking care of yourself is to create a list of ten daily habits.

These do not have to be major things, but they are a list of things that will make your life better and support you in taking care of yourself. Doing ten daily habits will give you a routine that will keep you focused, clear, motivated and healthy. When choosing your ten daily habits, choose those things that you really want, not things you think you should do or have to do. Your daily habits should get you jazzed up, be something that you really enjoy and look forward to doing.

Some of the daily habits I have established in my life are taking Prasad for a twenty minute walk everyday, playing with him for at least fifteen minutes twice a day, meditating for 20 minutes a day, keeping a daily journal, eating at least five fruits and veggies a day, taking a daily vitamin and laughing at least 10 times a day. These are things that I like to do and that make me feel great.

To start forming ten daily habits, start out slow. Choose only one or two to start with, do them for a month until they truly become habits and then add a couple more every month until you are up to ten, or whatever number feels good to you. And remember, these are not carved in stone, if you try out a habit that just does not work, dump it and find something you really like.

This is about taking care of yourself and doing what you want to do for yourself. Remember these are your habits, not anyone else's. By establishing ten daily habits you are creating a healthy routine that will support you in staying focused, give you more energy, and make you feel great.

Creating the life we really want is all about taking control. It is about deciding to make conscious choices in our lives, living each moment as if it were the most important. Eliminating tolerations and getting complete will free up energy in our lives. And taking extreme self care will keep us healthy and happy. Combining these principles can be the building blocks on which we create the life we truly want.

From Complaints To Commitments

What Do You Need At Work In Order To Thrive?

"We never have a chance to really talk about the big picture of our work. We're under so much pressure to deliver what is needed now. There's little opportunity to understand how things tie in with larger goals; consequently, there's no breathing space for creativity or innovation."

"I'd be able to grow and develop at work if I didn't have to be "Mom" or "Dad" around here...if my subordinates didn't come to me for every little decision and if they would take more initiative, I'd be freer to do the same in my own job."

"There's too much talking behind one's back here. People talk about others, but rarely to others. I don't feel people come to me directly; I find out about things from other people. If I knew and had a chance to talk to the person with a complaint, then we could confront the issues and work on solutions."

The objects of disaffections may vary. When things go from bad to worse the discussions end up in the manager's office. When they don't, they form an undercurrent of discontent and resentment that is counter-productive.

People spend vast amounts of time complaining. They even invest amazingly creative energies coming up with clever ways of expressing their discontent. No matter how sophisticated, however, a complaint is unpleasant to listen to. It can instill an aura of negativity and cynicism. It becomes contagious. At its worst, it poisons relationships and sabotages team efforts.

A review of journals and books yields little on the subject. Ask any group of people how they could be more supported at work and you'll get prime examples of it. Sometimes the complaints are made with head-shaking amusement, sometimes resentment and resignation. They are made by people who love their jobs, hate their jobs; by those that are good at their jobs, not so good, new at work, and near retirement. Criticisms are levied at bosses, subordinates, peers, "them," and occasionally at oneself.

We all complain, no matter what our position. No matter what the particular content of complaints, it turns out that most of us have an experience at work that we perceive as obstructing our own well-being, growth, and development.

This conversation about what we can't stand is so universal it goes unrecognized and accepted as normal. Obviously the use of this language form is more recognized in others than in ourselves. Complaining grows like a weed. The problem is that it does not usually lead to changing anything.

To be fair, complaining may help people let off steam. It can also create alliances and support when one realizes one is not alone, but it rarely accomplishes more than this. It doesn't transform anyone or anything. It often leaves people feeling worse by virtue of the negative feelings that flourish.

Why Complaints Are Important.

It is important to pay attention to complaints because they contain a seed of passion! For every statement of what a person can't stand, there is an underlying reason or statement about what they stand for.

Where there is passion there is possibility for transformation. There is energy and there is commitment. People do not complain about what they don't care about. So underneath the complaint, there is a river of committed passion and a source of energy to be discovered and harnessed...if we look for it and ask about it!

Leaders and managers are faced with complaints all the time. Here are some typical responses:

1. Acknowledge the person's complaint and give them more information that would explain the situation and provide another perspective.
2. Acknowledge the person's complaint by actively listening and empathizing with them in order to help them to accept the situation.

3. Acknowledge their complaint and try to explore solutions using problem-solving methods.

Depending on your leadership style, you will direct or coach them to take action, or you might take the monkey on yourself by agreeing to do something to fix the problem.

What if there was a different approach to handling complaints, one that actually encouraged people to stay with the problem in order to pursue meaningful transformation?

Kegan and Lahey suggest asking this important question:

What sorts of things, if they were to happen more frequently in your work setting, would you experience as being more supportive of your own ongoing development at work?

Transforming the language of complaints to the language of commitments

What commitments or convictions do you hold that are implied in your complaint? What value do you hold that is not being honored? What commitment do you have that is not being fully recognized by this situation?

In every complaint there is a value that is not being honored and it is usually the absence of this personal value that is rubbing the person the wrong way. Hence the passion that is implicit in complaints. Unlock the underlying value and there is productive conversation about what needs to be done in order to create meaningful change.

What if leaders could feel comfortable enough to listen to a complaint without explaining, empathizing, and trying to solve the problem? What if they took the time to explore for the unfulfilled values and commitments inherent in the BMW talk?

The world of complaints is highly popular at work. Rather than seeing them as problems to be solved, dissolved, suppressed, and squashed, however, Kegan and Lahey present an invitation and a challenge to leaders to make use of their energies. Complaints might be seen as a gateway to identifying and giving voice to personal commitments at work. It is a way to identify what people stand for, not just what they can't stand.

Work settings are language communities in that, structure, boundaries, norms, and culture are organized linguistically. The importance of language and the way groups speak about themselves and their work cannot be underemphasized. In that sense all leaders are leading language communities. Though every person, in any setting has some opportunity to influence the nature of the language, leaders have exponentially greater access and opportunity to establish and influence others through the use of language.

The only question is what kind of language leaders will choose to use.

Equally important is the language we use in our self-talk. Although too rarely considered, the conversation within is one of the most influential forces of behavioral regulation. Through our internal language, we create continuous forms of feelings and thoughts that ultimately lead to our actions. When you consider the three internal operating systems of feelings, thoughts, and language, language is the easiest to change.

When we change the way we talk about something, we have a greater chance of changing our feelings and thoughts because of our natural desire to be congruent. Ultimately, our behaviors change because we have changed the way we think, feel, and talk. To be inconsistent between these systems creates cognitive dissonance – that uncomfortable feeling of not "walking the talk."

The authors point out that leadership is a widespread phenomenon in business: "For every chief executive presiding at the top of some organization or enterprise, there are a thousand men and women called upon to exercise temporary or sustained leadership over a project or team within an organization."

Furthermore, leadership is about supporting and helping communities (organizations and teams) change through the use of language. It is with the language we use that we manage our relationships with each other and with organizations.

We are all leaders at one time or in one way. We are all challenged by being stuck and blocked from creating changes that we say are important to us. We are all seeking language through which we can communicate more effectively and influence the decisions that others make, particularly when they relate to what is important to us.

The fact is that all of us are confronted with challenges when it comes to development and change. While it may be that sometimes this is because we have difficulty learning something or we attach a loss to shifting to something new, in all cases it is because we are committed to something. There is something we value that we are protecting.

In the world of business and organizations this protective behaviour often shows up as complaining and various forms of discontent. It depletes work energy, negatively impacts retention of talented people, and at its extreme breeds anti-organizational behaviour such as sabotage.

Leading change through changing the language we use

Below, we have presented Kegan and Lahey's conceptual grid for making meaning out of complaints. The use of this model for exploring complaints is a valuable tool for leaders. Working through one's own complaints can help executives to a deeper understanding of the multiple meanings that must be recognized before transformational change can occur. We reprint them here with permission from the authors.

Step One: Write down your answers to the following question: "**What sorts of things, if they were to happen more frequently in your work setting, would you experience as being more supportive of your own ongoing development at work?**"

Step Two: Pick just one you feel strongly about and complete the following sentence... "**I am committed to the value or the importance of...**" for example, if your answer to step one was "I don't get feedback" then "I am committed to getting feedback."

Step Three: Consider your own part in the situation, by answering this question: "**What am I doing or not doing that prevents my commitment from being fully realized?**"

Step Four: Consider that you may have other values that are competing with your column 1 value or commitment: "I **may also be committed to...**" (this is usually something self-protective.)

For example, "I am also committed to not being vulnerable."

Step Five: Asks you to look at the reasons for holding the competing value stated in column 3 by finishing the statement: "**I assume that if...**" (if I do honour my commitment in col. 1, then this might mean....)

Column 1	**Column 2**	**Column 3**	**Column 4**
Recognizing a commitment or value hidden within a complaint	Personal Responsibility: What I am doing or not doing that prevents my commitment from being fully realized. . .	Recognizing a Competing Commitment or value	Big Assumption
I am committed to the value or the importance of. . .		I may also be committed to. . .	

To bring about actual change, we must do more than just become aware of our paradoxes. We must disturb the balance, not merely look at it. This map creates a more complete and comprehensive space in which to consider and experience a problem. Far from solving the problem, we expand it.

Why? For one thing, it will prevent us from wasting time, energy, and money on solutions that might be highly ineffective because the problems will just recur in differing forms.

On a psychological level, we create movement from subject to object... the movement of our meaning making is from a place where we are its captive to a place where we can look at it, reexamine it, and possibly alter it. This is what leads to genuine transformation.

Manage and Unleash Your Energy

The Idea in Brief

Organizations are demanding ever-higher performance from their workforces. People are trying to comply, but the usual method – putting in longer hours – has backfired. They're getting exhausted, disengaged, and sick. And they're defecting to healthier job environments.

Longer days at the office don't work because time is a limited resource. But personal energy is renewable, say Schwartz and McCarthy. By fostering deceptively simple rituals that help employees regularly replenish their energy, organizations build workers' physical, emotional, and mental resilience. These rituals include taking brief breaks at specific intervals, expressing appreciation to others, reducing interruptions, and spending more time on activities people do best and enjoy most.

Help your employees systematically rejuvenate their personal energy, and the benefits go straight to your bottom line. Take Wachovia bank: participants in an energy renewal program produced 13 percentage points greater year-to-year in revenues from loans than a control group did. And they exceeded the control group's gains in revenues from deposits by 20 percentage points.

The Idea in Practice

Schwartz and McCarthy recommend these practices for renewing four dimensions of personal energy:

Physical Energy

- Enhance your sleep by setting an earlier bedtime and reducing alcohol use.

- Reduce stress by engaging in cardiovascular activity at least three times a week and strength training at least once.
- Eat small meals and light snacks every three hours.
- Learn to notice signs of imminent energy flagging, including restlessness, yawning, hunger, and difficulty concentrating.
- Take brief but regular breaks, away from your desk, at 90- to 120-minute intervals throughout the day.

Emotional Energy

- Defuse negative emotions – irritability, impatience, anxiety, insecurity – through deep abdominal breathing.
- Fuel positive emotions in yourself and others by regularly expressing appreciation to others in detailed, specific terms through notes, e-mails, calls, or conversations.
- Look at upsetting situations through new lenses. Adopt a "reverse lens" to ask, "what would the other person in this conflict say, and how might he be right?" use a "long lens" to ask, "how will I likely view this situation in six months?" employ a "wide lens" to ask, "how can I grow and learn from this situation?"

Mental Energy

- Reduce interruptions by performing high-concentration tasks away from phones and e-mail.
- Respond to voice mails and e-mails at designated times during the day.
- Every night, identify the most important challenge for the next day. Then make it your first priority when you arrive at work in the morning.

Spiritual Energy

- Identify your "sweet spot" activities – those that give you feelings of effectiveness, effortless absorption, and fulfillment. Find ways to do more of these. One executive who hated doing sales reports delegated them to someone who loved that activity.

- Allocate time and energy to what you consider most important. For example, spend the last 20 minutes of your evening commute relaxing, so you can connect with your family once you're home.
- Live your core values. For instance, if consideration is important to you but you're perpetually late for meetings, practice intentionally showing up five minutes early for meetings.

How Companies Can Help

To support energy renewal rituals in your firm:

- Build "renewal rooms" where people can go to relax and refuel.
- Subsidize gym memberships.
- Encourage managers to gather employees for midday workouts.
- Suggest that people stop checking e-mails during meetings.

Section V

Add the Juice to The Dry Lemons:

- Accept What Can't Be Changed and Change What Can Be
- Dealing With Failure
- Lacking The Human Touch: Get it back.
- Maslow And The War Of Independence
- Empty Your Cup
- The Root Problem Of All The Problems
- Living For The Last Luxury

Accept What Can't Be Changed and Change What Can Be

"Your life is the sum result of all the choices you make, both consciously and unconsciously. If you can control the process of choosing, you can take control of all aspects of your life. You can find the freedom that comes from being in charge of yourself."

– M.K. Gandhi.

Accepting responsibility for choices starts with understanding where our choices lie. This idea is wonderfully framed by the timeless wisdom of the ancient Serenity Prayer:

God, grant me the serenity to accept the things I cannot change,
The courage to change the things I can,
And the wisdom to know the difference.

Each line represents an important step in growing our leadership. Consider the first – an invocation to "grant me the serenity to accept the things I cannot change."

There is a long list of things we as leaders can't control, but may have a major impact on our organizations. These include economic and political trends, technological changes, shifts in consumer preferences and market trends, as well as catastrophes wrought by human beings (war, terrorism) and so-called "Acts of God," such as hurricanes or tornadoes. The poet Longfellow offers great leadership counsel about how to handle these non-controllables when he says, "The best thing one can do when it is raining is to let it rain." Pretty solid advice!

The fact is that stuff happens. Life isn't fair. Whatever hits the fan certainly won't be evenly distributed. The best approach to dealing with things that cannot be changed is to accept them. The worst thing we can do is to succumb to the Victimitis Virus and "awfulize" the situation by throwing pity parties in Pity City. When the doo-doo starts to pile deep, a leader doesn't just sit there and complain (usually about "them"); he or she grabs a shovel. We may not choose what happens to us, but we do choose how to respond – or not.

The second line of the Serenity Prayer asks for "the courage to change the things I can." This is the gulp-and-swallow part. Choosing to make changes is hard. It's so much easier to blame everyone else for my problems and to use this as an excuse for doing nothing. But leaders don't give away their power to choose. In his bestseller, *The Road Less Traveled*, Scott Peck writes, "Whenever we seek to avoid the responsibility for our own behaviour, we do so by attempting to give that responsibility to some other individual or organization or entity.

But this means we then give away our power to that entity, be it 'fate' or 'society' or the government or the corporation or our boss. It is for this reason that Erich Fromm so aptly titled his study of Nazism and authoritarianism, *Escape from Freedom.* In attempting to avoid the pain of responsibility, millions and even billions daily attempt to escape from freedom."

It takes real courage to accept full responsibility for our choices – especially for our attitude and outlook. This is the beginning and ultimately most difficult act of leadership.

The concluding line of the Serenity Prayer – "and the wisdom to know the difference" – is perhaps the toughest part of all. In our workshops with management teams we often get into lively debates about those things over which the group has the power to act. We attempt to classify them as belonging to three categories: No Control; Direct Control; and Influence. It's rarely black and white.

For example, we often underestimate the influence we might have in our organizations – or in the world at large. But as Robert Kennedy once put it, "Each time a man stands up for an idea, or acts to improve the lot of others, or strikes out against injustice, he sends forth a tiny ripple of hope, and crossing each other from a million different centers of energy and daring, those ripples build a current that can sweep down the mightiest walls of oppression and resistance."

We're either part of the problem or part of the solution. There is no neutral ground. Strong leaders make the choice to be part of the solution and get on with it – no matter how small their ripples of change may be.

Dealing with Failure

Thomas Edison (1847–1931) is credited with the invention of the phonograph and the electric light bulb. When asked about his numerous experimental failures, he said: "I have not failed 700 times. I have not failed once. I have succeeded in proving that those 700 ways will not work. When I have eliminated the ways that will not work, I will find the way that will work." Whether this is apocryphal or not, it nonetheless conveys the message that "failure" is just a matter of perspective!

More recently, Edward de Bono said "It is better to have enough ideas for some of them to be wrong, than to be always right by having no ideas at all."

Most of us believe we're judged by our successes and failures, and that there's some disgrace associated with "failure." Yet if we look around us, we see many examples of peoples' failures bringing value to our lives. For example, in 1938 one Roy Plunkett, a research chemist at DuPont's Laboratories, "fell upon" Teflon, a surface coating whose applications now range from the aerospace industry to the kitchen. Dynamite, Velcro, Cellophane, and Post-it Notes are other examples of "failures" becoming hero products.

So, how can we cope with "failure?"

What You Need to Know

I've been job hunting for over six months now but with little success. At what point do I concede failure and give up?

It is often said that we give up on our dreams just one moment before they are fulfilled. Persistence seems to be the key, as is a very clear idea of what we wish to achieve. So, if finding new position is really what you want, keep at it a little while longer. You never know how close you are to hitting the jackpot! If you are not doing it already, ask the employers who have turned you down if they can give you any feedback on your application or interview performance, so that you can work on any areas that are letting you down. Remember, once you decide to give up, you have also given up on your chance of succeeding.

I feel so disheartened about a series of recent failures that I can't seem to find the energy to try again. What can I do to get myself focused again after these setbacks?

Focusing on the past and worrying about the way things have turned out is not a productive use of your creative energy. There is nothing you can do to change these experiences, but you can "reframe" them in other words, look at them from a different perspective. See them as learning experiences and reflect on what you can do differently another time. Be curious about what happened and why rather than judging yourself for being unable: you can learn those skills and by knowing where you went wrong, you can actively avoid those pitfalls next time around.

I am tackling a risky but important project and my name is bound up in its success. If the project doesn't deliver, what can I do to ensure I am not perceived as a failure?

It sounds as if this is a high-visibility enterprise. You might think through the different outcome scenarios and create some contingency plans that will enable you to pick things up credibly if any of them should come to fruition. This will make you appear to be in command of the situation. Managing expectations early on with key stakeholders your boss, say, or clients, colleagues, or other interested parties is also a good option. If you are running into problems, alert other people to the situation and explain what your approach is. That gives them the opportunity to pitch in with help if they feel it is appropriate, and you have also covered your back.

What to Do

Coping with failure is an art as well as the sign of a robust personality. Most of us fear failure because we do not want to risk feeling incompetent, useless, and foolish. However, by looking failure full in the face, you are courting the greatest success. Try celebrating the fact that you are willing to put yourself on the line for something you believe in and play for high stakes. You never know when one of your projects will pay off and enhance your reputation significantly.

Here are some ideas for preventing failure in the first place.

Have Positive Expectations: Envisage a positive outcome rather than a negative one. If you focus on your worst fears you may manifest them, so run the desired successful scenario through your mind with the intention that this is the one that will come to fruition. This is not about being in denial, but creating a positive environment where the likelihood of the best outcome is increased.

Be Proactive: Do not wait for things to run away with you until you are forced to act. If things are going off the rails, intervene as soon as you think it is necessary in order to straighten them out. Problems will not go away by themselves, so the sooner you act, the sooner a solution will be found.

See "Failure" As Part of the Creative Process

Just as Edison did, look at your creative endeavours as part of a bigger picture and allow the intrinsic successes and failures of the creative process take on their proper proportion in relation to the totality of what you are trying to achieve.

Take a Risk: Playing safe means that you will probably repeat past achievements, but it also means that you are unlikely to gain any new successes. What is the worst that can happen? Can any mistakes you make really be that bad in the grand schemes of things? If not, and you can live with them, why not give a new approach a try?

Be Disciplined, Dedicated, and Determined: In the worlds of film and music, we often see examples of so-called "overnight" success. What we do not see is the discipline, dedication, and determination that have enabled someone to reach their aspirations. Success is a hard slog, even though the media would have us believe that it can be gained instantly and without effort. You need to rally and focus your energies in order to succeed in the long run and then you can claim your rightful satisfaction and celebrate!

Make Clear Choices: Often, we have to choose one path over another in order to meet our goals. This isn't always a cut and dried decision, as many of us like to "hedge our bets" just in case one path does not lead us to where we want to go. Trying to use two approaches once only divides resources and halves our ability to succeed, however. You run the risk of falling between two opposing sets of objectives and end up achieving less than you might otherwise have done. You may have to sacrifice a lesser dream in order to achieve a greater one!

Be Decisive: Take "Active" Decisions: If you allow the ebbs and flows of your project to guide you, you will merely be presiding over the process as a passive observer. Even if you decide not to do something, make sure you've consciously chosen that path rather than just given up and let things happen to you. "Active"choices are so much more powerful than "passive" ones and they will make sure you remain engaged and influential.

Make Contingency Plans: Think about what you would do if your fears materialize so that you're not caught on the hop. Run different scenarios through your mind and imagine yourself dealing with these in an assertive and confident way. Preparing yourself in this way will ensure that you know what to do, whatever the eventuality.

If the worst does happen, there are plenty of useful strategies you can use for coping with failure.

Face Your Fears: Knowing yourself well helps you manage the ups and downs of your achievements. Try to understand what "failure" means to you. According to the communicational framework of transactional analysis (TA), we have five drivers: be perfect, hurry up, be strong, please others, and try hard.

One of these drivers may be responsible for your sense of failure. If, for example, you are driven by a need to be "perfect", failure will hit you hard because the driver central to your sense of well-being and confidence has been thwarted. Once you understand your own weak spots, you can identify coping strategies that will help you move through your sense of failure quickly.

Ask for Feedback: If you are bewildered by your lack of success, find a trusted friend or colleague to ask for feedback. You may learn something about yourself that you did not know. We often unconsciously sabotage ourselves by making assumptions and acting upon them as if they were the truth\but they may not be true for other people.

Create Coping Strategies: If you know that not getting things right all the time affects you badly, think of the ways you could be assisted or comforted if things do not go according to the plan. You might like to find a sounding board or coach who will help you think things through. You might like to arm yourself with a set of positive affirmations or a place to go that will remind you what you really care about and give you a sense of perspective.

Perhaps you like walking in nature and thinking alone, or maybe you enjoy taking part in group activities. Whatever your preferences, create a menu of activities you can call on to support you in these moments. Neuro-linguistic programming (NLP) is a behavioral framework that may help you understand your inner landscape and find coping strategies to help you through.

Find Something to Do That You Know You Are Good At: You might like to remind yourself of your worth by doing something at which you excel: anything from cooking to art, sport, music, you name it. Spend some time doing this to refresh your confidence and give you the boost of energy you will need to try again.

Remember, it is not you who has failed, merely an experiment you were conducting!

What to Avoid

You Worry You Look Like a Fool:

Failing in some capacity often means that we are introduced to our vulnerabilities, and we may feel exposed, embarrassed, and a bit of a fool. No one would willingly look for that type of outcome, but by holding ourselves back and not risking failure, we are keeping ourselves small.

We are not really living if we try to protect ourselves from trying new things: you will not fail, but you will not succeed at anything either. To spur you on, think of the times that you have taken a risk and it has paid off. Remember that feeling of pride and achievement.

You Take It Personally: Failure is not about "you" as a person, but how you interact with the world. None of us gets everything right all the time, but it does not mean we are not successful human beings. Try to distance yourself from the personal impact that your failures may have and be objective about your experiences. In this way, you can learn from them and try something different another time.

You Focus On Failure: Sometimes we are so fearful of failure that we unwittingly make it our goal. We know that if goals are set clearly and measurably, whether they be positive or negative, our energy is directed at meeting them.

If we focus on failure, it creeps into our subconscious mind as a goal, and we find ourselves creating the conditions for it to happen. To avoid this, discipline yourself to focus on the positive outcome so that your success is manifested, not your failure.

You Will Not Change Your Approach: Albert Einstein once defined insanity as "doing the same thing over and over again and expecting different results." If your approach is not working, try something else.

You Lose Patience: We often get impatient and seek short cuts or compromises when we are unable to reach our goals. Do not reduce your goals in response to your impatience. Keep your eye on what you really want and remember that discipline, dedication, and determination are necessary if you want a worthwhile success.

Lacking the Human Touch

When given a list of a dozen words to describe their CEO, only one in five employees picked "caring" or "warm." (Small wonder that these words were picked twice as often by the CEOs asked to describe their own attributes.) In addition, nearly half of all employees surveyed gave the top boss a grade of C, D, or F for both compassion and communication. In terms of people skills, bosses are falling well short of the mark.

Top Likes and Dislikes

Managers appreciate CEO's vision. Communication style? Not so much.

"This is a real problem," says Rafael Pastor, CEO of Vistage International, a networking organization for CEOs. "CEOs do not do a good enough job of inspiring their employees and making them feel important and valuable. Their soft skills are not as finely honed as their other business skills."

Bad marks in these categories didn't surprise Bob Sutton, a professor of Management Science at Stanford and author of the recent book, "*The no asshole rule: Building a civilized workplace and surviving one that isn't.*" There is plenty of research in social psychology that indicates that when you give people power, they become more focused on their needs and less on those of people around them, he says. Power tends to turn people into jerks.

There are a variety of ways for a CEO to improve his or her interpersonal skills, but most revolve around this simple advice: if you are the CEO, you need to step out of the corner office and get more face time with the people who work for you. This clearly shows that employees who interact regularly with their CEOs had a significantly higher opinion of their job performance.

"If you're getting bad evaluations in these soft skills, the first thing I would ask is, how much personal contact are you having with your employees?" Management professor William Wallick says. "If you are not a personal presence in the lives of your employees, they are likely to form their impression from the stories they hear at the water cooler. Unfortunately, the grapevine traffics in bad news. People don't gossip about the moments when the boss was a nice guy. What people talk about are the moments when the CEO messes up or behaves badly."

Several experts warned that suddenly morphing into a nice guy isn't likely to pass the smell test with the rank and file. Don't try to fake a new warmth of character unless that is a true reflection of your personality. "The best advice is not changing your interpersonal behaviour but simply having more of it on display," says David Gliddon, a researcher in business innovation and a faculty member of Colorado Technical University.

Management-by-walking-around doesn't end with handshakes and the pats on the back. If the feedback that the CEO gets from lower level employees doesn't become part of the decision-making process, employees will come to believe that the glad-handing is a sham.

Others point out, too, that it is very possible for a CEO to become too concerned with his or her popularity among the employees. "It is not a CEO's job to be liked," says author Michael Abrashoff. "The CEO is responsible for results, but you can't get results unless you have the respect of those who work for you. Gaining employees' respect is necessary for doing business, but simply being liked should not be on any CEO's to-do list."

"There are a lot of ineffectual nice guys out there," Pastor agrees. "Being liked is not necessarily going to solve the criticism of your employees. They want to know the CEO is effective and that they are going to do the right thing by the employee."

Indeed, the different perspectives of the CEO and the employee may explain some of the differences of opinions. "There is a strong component of selfishness in the employees' evaluation of their boss," says Pastor. "The employee is likely assessing their boss largely on whether the employee feels valued and properly rewarded. The employee wants to know: Does the CEO spend enough time with me? Do I have a way to move up in the organization?"

Chief executives, on the other hand, must juggle the demands of several constituencies at once. The CEO has to manage employees but also answer to shareholders and board of directors. They have to be an advocate for the customer as well as watch out for competition. These different pulls for attention and resources may mean that one or more of these groups feel ignored at times, all of which is to say that some disconnect between employee and CEO assessment is just part of the job.

There's another justifiable reason why CEOs tend to overestimate their abilities and attributes. All eyes are on the CEO all the time, and a baseline level of self-confidence is a prerequisite for the job. "You should have a leader who errs on the side of optimism about their own abilities," says Sutton. "No one wants a CEO who expresses crippling self-doubt the moment things go wrong. You have to act like you're in charge even when you don't know what is going on. Sometimes you have to fake it until you make it."

Perhaps the most disturbing CEO "blind spot" we found was the topic of innovation. CEOs and their employees disagreed dramatically as to whether good ideas bubbled up through the bureaucracy of an organization. Only a third of employees thought that good ideas found their way up through the organization to the CEO, and almost a quarter believed that good ideas never or rarely made it from the cubicle to the executive suite. Remarkably, the vast majority of CEOs thought their organizations were doing well in this regard.

The Idea Trap

Managers are especially critical of how CEOs seek out good ideas from the management ranks.

"This result is not a matter of two disagreeing opinions. The fact that those two assessments are so far apart means that something is wrong in the organization," says Management Professor William Wallick. "It's critical that CEOs don't rely on their gut feelings on this issue. If you're not sure whether the paths of communication are open, you need to get out of your office and find out by talking with employees up and down the organizational chart."

Most CEOs would like to believe they're open to "innovation", it's the business watchword of our age. According to management professor Bob Sutton, however, few executives actually understand what it takes to be tackle change head-on. "For true innovation to happen, employees have to be able to take [a] risk and fail. They also have to feel that they are free to speak out," says Sutton. "Executives may talk a lot about innovation but at the same time punish the employees who go out on a limb."

Sutton also notes that over-involvement from management may have a negative effect. "When you plant a seed in the ground, you don't dig it up every week to see how it is doing," he says. "CEOs who are constantly looking over the shoulder of those who are trying to come up with new approaches often just get in the way."

Several experts point out that employees and CEOs may be answering a slightly different question when it comes to innovation. Employees, after all, aren't just concerned with good ideas being recognized for the benefit of the organization, they also want credit for those ideas. An organization that has its ears open to new ideas but rarely rewards employees for generating them undoubtedly will get bad marks on this question.

Another reason for the disparity: Employees often don't get feedback on ideas that aren't adopted. By their nature, businesses can only adopt a small percentage of change-making ideas, lest they rewrite the business plan every week. For this reason, it is just as important to let employees know why an idea isn't being adopted as it is to give them credit when an idea is implemented.

"If you don't get any feedback when you suggest an idea, you become cynical," author Michael Abrashoff says. "Lack of negative feedback communicates the impression that the ideas aren't being heard. Giving a clear reason why an idea isn't going to be adopted is better than silence."

The lukewarm evaluations of CEOs also may point to a generation gap between typically baby boomer-era upper management and Gen X- and Gen Y-age employees and managers. Several experts pointed out that the younger employees expect a more nurturing, less autocratic style of leadership.

"The old days of command and control are gone," says Vistage International CEO Rafael Pastor. "A CEO can't rely on the strength of his corporate structure to make things happen. Younger employees expect a level of collaboration and communication that their parents didn't expect."

Author Michael Abrashoff adds, "Today's younger generation requires a new set of managerial skills. They want to know why you are doing things in a certain way and will only buy into a project if they understand why you are doing what you're doing."

This doesn't mean that Generation X and Y employees aren't capable of being great team players or that they don't care about the company. When asked what they would like to discuss with their CEO if they had the chance, employees young and old showed a remarkable degree of selflessness. More than half said that they wanted to chat with the top boss about the company's long-term vision or strategy. Less than one in four wanted to talk with the CEO about their personal career prospects or their salaries.

When asked what qualities they thought their CEO valued most, the vast majority of employees young and old chose answers like "integrity," "delivering results," "innovative thinking," "honesty," and "resourcefulness." Fewer than one in 10 believed CEOs were impressed by smooth talkers or suck-ups.

Maslow And The War Of Independence

"I must study politics and war that my sons may have liberty to study mathematics and philosophy. My sons ought to study mathematics and philosophy, geography, natural history, naval architecture, navigation, commerce, and agriculture, in order to give their children a right to study painting, poetry, music, architecture, statuary, tapestry, and porcelain."

Now you may be very familiar with this quotation. I was (perhaps to my shame) not so familiar and I enjoyed it. Part of my enjoyment was that John Adams pre-dates Abraham Maslow by almost 200 years. In fact, this John Adams lived 1735-1826 and was the second president of the United States 1797-1801. (I hope that I have the right one. John Quincy Adams, the sixth president of the United States, lived 1767-1848.)

Now you will recall that Maslow argues for a hierarchy of needs from physiological through security, social and esteem needs to the need for self-actualisation. Adams seems to be saying the very same thing. In fact, a variation of Maslow's hierarchy was proposed by Bill Reddin. He inserted the need for independence into the hierarchy after esteem (which he called "respect") and before self-actualization.

It may at first seem to be a bad pun to say that John Adams almost certainly had independence in mind – but perhaps it is not. After all, the American Revolution was very much about self-determination, even if it started as a row over taxes. Independence, as Bill Reddin said, is a pre-condition of self-actualization.

So Adams' words might be translated as "I seek security so that my sons can seek independence in order that their children may seek self-actualization." Thus, Maslow's hierarchy can be seen to be a description not only of the motivation of individuals but also of society or at least democratic society as Adams says. (perhaps I ought to rename it Adams' hierarchy. He came first!)

The social and historical context

So what is the truth of Adams' words in a social or historical context? Clearly, following the war of independence, the USA enjoyed a long period when it progressed towards the major economic power it is today, a period interrupted only by the civil war. Clearly today, it is the society most given to concerns for self-actualization.

Other societies have not progressed as far towards Adams' third developmental stage – some fixed in a state of conflict, others seeking economic independence and still others at what Adams might have termed a pre-stage, a continuing and sometimes desperate struggle for survival, Maslow's physiological need. You could argue that the society's most resembling the USA in its concerns for self-actualization are perhaps Holland (the Netherlands), Australia and Canada – or perhaps you have other ideas?

The problem with the global application of Maslow's hierarchy of needs has always seemed to me to be that it applies mainly to developed societies and then mainly to the wealthy or at least the comfortably-off in those societies. I do not mean that it is wrong but only that its application is limited.

However, the long period of relative peace that most of the world has enjoyed since the 50's has probably made concerns for self-actualization more possible for more people in more places than ever before. In my review of Covey's "*The 7 Habits of Highly Effective People*", I said that I hoped that such a book could be relevant post 9/11, that the concerns of whether school classes can be skipped for a tennis match would again become important to people. That hope is worth expressing again. (The fact remains that self-actualization matters only when safety exists and it does not do so everywhere.)

Changes in motivation

Nevertheless, given that "concerns for self-actualization are more possible for more people in more places than ever before", there are implications for business and for management. Indeed, in many societies with which I am acquainted – for example Eastern Europe, North America, Hong

Kong, Singapore, Australia and so on – graduates and others entering the workforce today seem less and less interested in business and organizations and their success as such, and more and more interested in personal relationships, involvement (in music, travel, film and theatre or having fun) and even "fame" – whether for fifteen minutes or more.

History and Time

Motivation and work, indeed the motivation to work, change during history and in many ways; one can use Maslow's (or Adams') hierarchy to categorize this. I have been reading Keith Wrightstown's book, "*English society 1580-1680.*" Talking about the degrees of people, he discusses income levels. A regularly employed labmyer, "in the south of England in the early seventeenth century might earn a maximum of around 10 8s a year" (10.40 in decimal coinage equivalent to about 15.6 Euros or us dollars.)

He goes on: "As for the costs of subsistence for an average family, various estimates suggest that around11-14 (16.5-21 Euros or US dollars) would be necessary for food, clothing, fuel and rent in normal years: substantially more in times of scarcity and high food prices." As he says, "... The glaring fact is that the life of the labmyer was a constant battle for survival." For such people, the motivation to find work was clear and the nature of the work mattered not at all.

To suggest that this motivation – survival – is not important today would be disingenuous. However, it is also true that for very many societies, such basic needs are easier to satisfy and it has become the nature of work and its relationship with the rest of life which is more important.

For many people, the creation of a decent standard of living (Adams' "navigation, commerce, and agriculture") is the purpose of their work. In Maslow's terms, I might think of this as the search for security. However, increasingly today people, and specifically younger people in developed societies, see even such security needs as relatively easy to achieve. Adams' list – "painting, poetry, music, architecture, statuary, tapestry, and porcelain – has become more important."

Old fashioned motivation

Now, what counts as a "decent standard of living" is only partly a mathematical construct. Indeed the search for greater and greater material ill-being is ultimately endless. No, what seems to be occurring is a feeling that "what I have is fine, thanks" and a decision to trade off greater material rewards for quality of, or more importantly value in, life. In such circumstances, the motivation to work becomes dramatically changed and the old-fashioned attempts by organizations to motivate their employees become hopelessly ill-conceived

Always been there

People seeking independence and a form of self-actualisation have perhaps always existed. In the past, however, such people represented a tiny minority of a society's population. They were the secure and wealthy ones. As Keith Wrightson reports:

"Gentlemen, taken together with their immediate families, constituted a tiny minority of the English population – around 2 per cent ... in the early seventeenth century."

The "gentlemen" and their dependants, of course, constituted the leisured class and while not calling modern "knowledge workers" a leisured class, they at least are not wholly dependent upon the good will of any one employer for the satisfaction of their physiological and security needs.

So given that what I have called "old-fashioned" methods of motivation will no longer work for an increasing number of people, the implication is that the perhaps equally "old-fashioned" type of organization will less and less attract the brightest and best (and the most independent and self-actualizing.) How do we create organizations that will motivate them?

Surely an implication is that large power differentials, insistence on status and top down decision making have had their day. They reinforce the idea that employees are there to do what they are told – and the best and brightest will simply reject this notion. It does not fit with their worldview, their values of independence nor does it lead to opportunities for anything resembling self-actualization.

The Answer

So what is the answer? To some extent, Herzberg has given it already and it is interesting to see how Maslow and Herzberg come together at this point. As you will recall, distinguishing motivating factors from hygiene factors, as we say elsewhere:

"Motivation, says Herzberg, derives from people having a sense of achievement, recognition, responsibility and opportunities for personal growth."

WHY IS THIS SO DIFFICULT TO LEARN? WELL, AS WE ALSO SAY ELSEWHERE:

"*Many managers find it difficult to deal with the Herzberg's motivators, perhaps because they imply genuinely working with people, their desires, ambitions and personalities.*"

It is really about time that managers learned that management is more about people and less about systems and procedures and certainly less about "rank implying knowledge." The modern organization needs the creativity, commitment and imagination of its people – now more than ever – and such an organization is not formed from top down management.

How do you motivate people?

I am frequently asked the somewhat disturbing question, "Well, how do you motivate people then?" The question is disturbing because it implies that the questioner thinks there is a quick and ready answer and also because it seems to imply that the questioner has been failing to do it to date. I often reply by asking why they think people at the top of organizations or entrepreneurs seem so motivated.

The answer to that question is quite straightforward. For people at the top and for entrepreneurs, there is little distinction between work and play. They express themselves in their work or their roles. The organization's successes are their successes and thus (largely) their self-actualization.

So how do you motivate people lower in the organization? Well, you create an organization in which everyone can feel that "the organization's successes are their successes." This implies putting Herzberg's words into practice, concentrating upon creating an organization that offers enjoyment, personal growth, achievement and responsibility.

More than this, and going beyond Herzberg in the direction of Anita Roddick, organizations need to have values that people can genuinely accept and adopt as their own. Profitability matters – of course it does – but it matters not as the end point but as the means. As Matsushita-san said, "profit is the reward for correct behaviour" and as Luis Bastias says "money plays the very same role (for organizations) that air plays for the existence of living beings."

Long term success – continued existence being dependent upon a supply of oxygen – demands values in organizational life. Without them, the organization will not attract and maintain the brightest and best – who will feel that they can go elsewhere even at a lower salary (which will bother them less than feeling alienated by the organization.) Values have changed.

Motivation and society

As I have said, the truth of this depends upon the nature of the society in which the organization exists. Maybe there is no one path that all societies follow but there is at least a poetic truth in what Adams says. Organizations are, at the very least, not independent of the values of a society – though the brightest and best members of that society may make themselves independent of an organization which is not in tune with their values.

So the basic question of management becomes, "What form and culture of organization will offer the best and brightest the independence and self-actualization they demand, consistent with making sufficient profit to ensure the continued successful existence of the organization?" (A more courageous version of this question would substitute the words "consistent with making" by "in order to make.")

Such a form and culture comes along not by accident but by deliberate design and it is unfortunate that few leaders think this way. It is perhaps for this reason that so much management training in organizations exists in a vacuum – or to change the analogy, operates like a cogwheel unconnected with the other wheels in the organization.

Management training is primarily about showing people how to manage in a specific culture. If the words "in a specific culture" are missed out, the objective becomes fairly meaningless – and no, I am not arguing for classes in "painting, poetry, music, architecture, statuary, tapestry, and porcelain."

EMPTY YOUR CUP

The Japanese master Nan-in gave audience to a professor of philosophy. Serving tea, Nan-in filled his visitor's cup, and kept pouring. The professor watched the overflow until he could restrain himself no longer: "Stop! The cup is over full, no more will go in." Nan-in said: "Like this cup, you are full of your own opinions and speculations. How can I show you Zen unless you first empty your cup."

You have come to an even more dangerous person than Nan-in, because an empty cup won't do; the cup has to be broken completely. Even empty, if you are there, then you are full. Even emptiness fills you. If you feel that you are empty you are not empty at all, you are there. Only the

name has changed: now you call yourself emptiness. The cup won't do at all; it has to be broken completely.

Only when you are not can the tea be poured into you, only when you are not is there no need really to pour the tea into you. When you are not the whole existence begins pouring, the whole existence becomes a shower from every dimension, from every direction. When you are not, the divine is.

The story is beautiful. It was bound to happen to a professor of philosophy. The story says a professor of philosophy came to Nan-in. He must have come for the wrong reasons because a professor of philosophy, as such, is always wrong. Philosophy means intellect, reasoning, thinking, argumentativeness. And this is the way to be wrong, because you cannot be in love with existence if you are argumentative. Argument is the barrier. If you argue, you are closed; the whole existence closes to you. Then you are not open and existence is not open to you.

When you argue, you assert. Assertion is violence, aggression, and the truth cannot be known by an aggressive mind, the truth cannot be discovered by violence. You can come to know the truth only when you are in love. But love never argues. There is no argument in love, because there is no aggression. And remember, not only was that man a professor of philosophy, you are also the same. Every man carries his own philosophy, and every man in his own way is a professor, because you profess your ideas, you believe in them. You have opinions, concepts, and because of opinions and concepts your eyes are dull, they cannot see; your mind is stupid, it cannot know.

Ideas create stupidity, because the more the ideas are there the more the mind is burdened. And how can a burdened mind know? The more ideas there are the more it is just like dust which has gathered on a mirror. How can the mirror, mirror? How can the mirror reflect? Your intelligence is just covered by opinions the dust, and everyone who is opinionated is bound to be stupid and dull. That's why professors of philosophy are almost always stupid. They know too much to know at all. They are burdened too much. They cannot fly in the sky, they can't have wings. And they are so much in the mind; they can't have roots in the earth. They are not grounded in the earth and they are not free to fly into the sky.

And remember, you are all the same. There may be differences of quantity, but every mind is qualitatively the same, because mind thinks, argues, collects and gathers knowledge and becomes dull. Only children are intelligent. And if you can retain your childhood, if you continuously reclaim your childhood, you will remain innocent and intelligent. If you gather dust, childhood is lost, innocence is no more; the mind has become dull and stupid. Now you can have philosophies.

**The more philosophies you have,
the more you are far away from the divine.**

A religious mind is a non-philosophical mind. A religious mind is an innocent, intelligent mind. The mirror is clear, the dust has not been gathered; and every day a continuous cleaning goes on. That's what I call meditation.

This professor of philosophy came to Nan-in. He must have come for wrong reasons: he must have come to receive some answers. Those people who are filled with questions are always in search of answers. And Nan-in cannot give an answer. It is foolish to be concerned with questions and answers. Nan-in can give you a new mind, Nan-in can give you a new being, Nan-in can give you a new existence in which no questions arise. But Nan-in is not interested in answering any particular questions. He is not interested in giving answers. Neither am I.

You must have come here with many questions. It is bound to be so, because the mind gives birth to questions. Mind is a question-creating mechanism. Feed anything into it, out comes a question, and many questions follow. Give an answer to it; immediately it converts it into many questions. You are here, filled with many questions, your cup is already full. No need for Nan-in to pour any tea into it, you are already overflowing.

I can give you a new existence – that's why I have invited you here – I will not give you any answers. All questions, all answers are useless, just a wastage of energy. But I can transform you, and that is the only answer. And that one answer solves all questions.

Philosophy has many questions, many answers – millions. Religion has only one answer; whatsoever the question the answer remains the same. Buddha used to say: You taste sea water from anywhere, the taste remains the same, the saltiness of it.

Whatsoever you ask is really irrelevant. I will answer the same because I have got only one answer. But that one answer is like a master key; it opens all doors. It is not concerned with any particular lock – any lock and the key opens it. Religion has only one answer and that answer is meditation. Meditation means how to empty yourself.

The professor must have been tired, walking long, when he reached Nan-in's cottage. And Nan-in said: "Wait a little." He must have been in a hurry. Mind is always in a hurry, and mind is always in search of instantaneous realizations. For the mind, to wait is very difficult, almost impossible. Nan-in said: "I will prepare tea for you. You look tired. Wait a little, rest a little, and have a cup of tea. And then we can discuss."

Nan-in boiled the water and started preparing the tea. But he must have been watching the professor. Not only was the water boiling, the professor was also boiling within. Not only was the tea kettle making sounds, the professor was making more sounds within, chattering, continuously talking. The professor must have been getting ready – what to ask, how to ask, from where to begin.

He must have been in a deep monologue. Nan-in must have been smiling and watching: This man is too full, so much so that nothing can penetrate into him. The answer cannot be given because there is no one to receive it. The guest cannot enter into the house – there is no room. Nan-in must have wanted to become a guest in this professor.

Out of compassion, a Buddha always wants to become a guest within you.

He knocks from everywhere but there is no door. And even if he breaks a door, which is very difficult, there is no room. You are so full with yourself and with rubbish and all types of furniture which you have gathered in many, many lives, you cannot even enter into yourself; there is no room, no space. You live just outside of your own being, just on the steps. You cannot enter within yourself, everything is blocked.

Then Nan-in poured tea into the cup. The professor became uneasy, because Nan-in was continuously pouring tea. It was overflowing; soon it would be going onto the floor. Then the professor said: "Stop! What are you doing? Now this cup cannot hold any more tea, not even a single drop. Are you mad? What are you doing?"

Nan-in said: "The same is the case with you. You are so alert to observe and become aware that the cup is full and cannot hold any more, why are you not so aware about your own self? You are overflowing with opinions, philosophies, doctrines, scriptures. You know too much already; I cannot give you anything. You have travelled in vain. Before coming to me you should have emptied your cup, then I could pour something into it."

But I tell you, you have come to a more dangerous person. No, an empty cup I won't allow, because if the cup is there you will fill it. You are so addicted and you have become so habituated that you cannot allow the cup to be empty even for a single moment. The moment you see emptiness anywhere you start filling it. You are so scared of emptiness, you are so afraid: emptiness appears like death. You will fill it with anything, but you will fill it. No, I have invited you to be here to break down this cup completely, so that even if you want to, you cannot fill it.

Emptiness means there is no cup left. All the walls have disappeared, the bottom has fallen down; you have become an abyss. Then I can pour myself into you. Much is possible, if you allow. But to allow is arduous, because to allow you will have to surrender. Emptiness means surrender.

Nan-in was saying to that professor: Bow down, surrender, empty your head. I am ready to pour. That professor had not even asked the question and Nan-in had given the answer, because really there is no need to ask the question. The question remains the same.

Whether you ask me or not, I know what the question is. So many of you are here but I know the question, because deep down the question is one: the anxiety, the anguish, the meaninglessness, the futility of this whole life – not knowing who you are. But you are filled. Allow me to break this cup. This camp is going to be a destruction, a death. If you are ready to be destroyed something new will come out of it. Every destruction can become a creative birth. If you are ready to die you can have a new life, you can be reborn.

I am here just to be a midwife. That's what Socrates used to say – that a master is just a midwife. I can help, I can protect, I can guide, that's all. The actual phenomenon, the transformation, is going to happen to you. Suffering will be there, because no birth is possible without suffering. Much anguish will come up, because you have accumulated it and it has to be thrown. A deep cleansing and catharsis will be needed.

Birth is just like death, but the suffering is worth taking.

Out of the darkness of suffering a new morning arises, a new sun arises. And the dawn is not very far off when you feel darkness too much. When suffering is unbearable, bliss is very near. So don't try to escape from suffering – that is the point where you can miss. Don't try to avoid it, pass through it. Don't try to find some way which goes round about – no, that won't do. Pass through it.

Suffering will burn you, destroy you, but really you cannot be destroyed. All that can be destroyed is just the rubbish that you have gathered. All that can be destroyed is something that is not you. When it is all destroyed, then you will feel that you are indestructible, you are deathless. Passing through death, consciously passing through death, one becomes aware of life eternal.

These few days you will be here with me many things are possible, but the first step to remember is to pass through suffering. Many times I create suffering for you; many times I create the situation in which all that is suppressed within you comes up. Don't push it down, don't repress it. Allow it, free it. If you can free your suffering, your suppressed suffering, you will become free of it. And you can come to the state of bliss only when all suffering has been passed through, thrown, completely dropped.

And I can see through you: the flame of bliss is just near the corner. Once a glimpse and that flame becomes yours. I will push you in many ways to have a glimpse of it. If you miss you will be responsible, no one else. The river is flowing, but if you cannot bow down, if you cannot come down from your egoistic state of mind, you may go back thirsty. Don't blame the river. The river was there but you were paralyzed by your ego.

That's what Nan-in says: Empty the cup. That means empty the mind. Ego is there, overflowing, and when ego is overflowing nothing can be done. The whole existence is around you but nothing can be done. All around the divine...surrounded...but nothing can be done. From nowhere can the divine penetrate youself. You have created such a citadel. Empty the cup. Rather, throw the cup completely. When I say throw the cup completely I mean be so empty that you don't have even the feeling that "I am empty."

Once it happened, a disciple camc to Bodhidharma and said: "Master, you told me to be empty. Now I have become empty. Now what else do you say?"

Bodhidharma hit him hard with his staff on the head, and he said: "Go and throw this emptiness out."

If you say: "I am empty," the "I am" is there, and the "I" cannot be empty. So emptiness cannot be claimed. No one can say: "I am empty," just as no one can say: "I am humble." If you say: "I am humble," you are not. Who claims this humility? Humbleness cannot be claimed. If you are humble, you are humble, but you cannot say it. Not only can you not say it, you cannot feel that you are humble because the very feeling will give birth to the ego again. Be empty, but don't think that you are empty, otherwise you have deceived yourself.

You have brought many philosophies with you.

Drop them. They have not helped you at all, they have not done anything for you. It is time enough, the right time. Drop them wholesale, not in parts, not in fragments. For these few days you will be here with me just be without any thinking. I know it is difficult but still I say it is possible. And once you know the knack of it, you will laugh at the whole absurdity of the mind that you were carrying so long.

I have heard about a man who was travelling in a train for the first time, a villager. He was carrying his luggage on his head, thinking: "Putting it down will be too much for the train to carry, and I have paid only for my own self. I have purchased the ticket but I have not paid for the luggage." So he was carrying the luggage on his head. The train was carrying him and his luggage, and whether he carried it on his head or put it down made no difference to the train.

Your mind is unnecessary luggage. It makes no difference to this existence that is carrying you; you are unnecessarily burdened. I say: Drop it. The trees exist without the mind and exist more beautifully than any human being; the birds exist without the mind and exist in a more ecstatic state than any human being. Look at children who are still not civilized, who are still wild.

They exist without the mind, and even a Jesus or a Buddha will feel jealous of their innocence. There is no need for this mind. The whole world is going on and on without it. Why are you carrying it? Are you just thinking that it will be too much for God, too much for existence? Once you can put it down, even for a single minute, your whole existence will be transformed. You will enter into a new dimension, the dimension of weightlessness.

That's what I'm going to give you: wings into the sky, into the heaven – weightlessness gives you these wings and roots into the earth, a grounding, a centering. This earth and that heaven: they are two parts of the whole. In this life, your so-called ordinary life, you must be rooted; and in your inner space, in the spiritual life, you must be weightless and flying and flowing, floating.

Roots and wings I can give to you, if you allow – because I am only a midwife. I cannot force the child out of you. A forced child will be ugly, and a forced child may die. Just allow me. The child is there, you are already pregnant. Everybody is pregnant with God. The child is there and you have already carried too long; long ago the period of nine months passed.

That may be the root cause of your anguish – that you are carrying something in the womb which needs birth, which needs to come out, which needs to be born. Think of a woman, a mother, carrying a child after the ninth month. Then it becomes more and more burdensome, and if the birth is not going to happen the mother will die, because it will be too much to bear. That may be the reason why you are in so much anxiety, anguish and tension. Something needs to be born out of you; something needs to be created out of your womb. I can help.

This Samadhi Sadhana Shibir, this camp for inner ecstasy and enlightenment, is just going to be a help for you so that which you have carried like a seed up to now can come out of your soil and become an alive thing, an alive plant. But the basic thing will be that if you want to be with me you cannot be with your mind. Both cannot happen simultaneously.

Whenever you are with your mind you are not with me;
Whenever you are with your mind you are not with me;
Whenever the mind is not there you are with me.

And I can work only if you are with me. Empty the cup. Throw the cup away completely; destroy it.

Only earth exists; you are not there. This is what I mean when I say break the cup completely: forget that you are. The earth is, dissolve into it.

Anoth r new thing: I will not be there; only my empty chair will be there. But don't miss me because in a sense I will be there, and in a sense there has always been an empty chair before you.

Right now the chair is empty because
there is no one sitting in it.

I have heard that Adolph Hitler was suffering from deep depression, melancholy, and psychologists were saying that it was due to some hidden inferiority complex. So all the Aryan psychologists were called. They tried but they couldn't help, nothing came out of their analysis. So they suggested that a Jewish psychoanalyst should be called.

Hitler was not ready in the beginning to call a Jew, but seeing no way out of it he had to yield. A great Jewish psychoanalyst was called. He analyzed, penetrated deep into Hitler's mind, dreams, and then he suggested: "nothing much is a problem. Simply repeat one thing continuously: 'I am important, I am significant, I am indispensable.' Let it be a mantra.

Night, day, whenever you remember, repeat: 'I am important, I am significant, I am indispensable.'"

Hitler said: "Stop! You are giving me bad advice." The psychoanalyst couldn't understand. He said: "What do you mean? Why do you call this bad advice?"

Hitler said: "Because whatsoever I say, I am such a liar I cannot believe it. I am such a liar, whatsoever I say I cannot believe. If you say: repeat 'I am indispensable,' I know that this is a lie. I am saying it. I am a liar."

Out of lies, if you repeat something it will become a lie; out of fear, if you do something it will become a fear again. Out of hate, if you try to love, that love will just be a hidden hate; it cannot be anything else you are full of hate. Go to the preachers and they will say: "try to love." They are talking nonsense because how can a person who is full of hate try to love? If he tries to love, this love will come out of hatred; it will be poisoned already, poisoned from the very source. And this is what the misery of all preachers is.

Gandhi said to people who were violent: try to be non-violent. Then their non-violence comes out of violence, so their non-violence is just a façade, just a face to show. Deep down, they are boiling with violence. If your brahmacharya, your celibacy, comes out of too much sexuality, it will be perverted sex, nothing else.

So please don't create any conflict.

If you have one problem, don't create another; remain with the one, don't fight and create another. It is easier to solve one problem than to solve another; and the first is near the source, the second will be removed. The further removed, the more impossible it becomes to solve it.

If you have fear, you have fear – why make a problem out of it? Then you know that you have fear, just as you have two hands. Why create a problem out of it – as if you have only one nose, not two? Why create a problem out of it? Fear is there: accept it, note it. Accept it, don't bother about it. What will happen? Suddenly you will feel it has disappeared.

And this is the inner alchemy – a problem disappears if you accept it, and a problem grows more and more complex if you create any conflict with it. Yes, suffering is there, and suddenly fear comes – accept it. It is there and nothing can be done about it. And when I say nothing can be done about it, don't think that I am talking to you about pessimism. When I say nothing can be done about it I am giving you the key to solve it.

Suffering is there. It is part of life and part of growth; nothing is bad in it. Suffering becomes evil only when it is simply destructive and not creative at all; suffering becomes bad only when you suffer and nothing is gained out of it. But I am telling you the divine can be gained through suffering; then it becomes creative. Darkness is beautiful if the dawn is coming out of it soon; darkness is dangerous if it is endless, leads to no dawn, simply continues and continues and you go on moving in a rut, in a vicious circle.

This is what is happening to you. Just to escape from one suffering you create another; then to escape from another, another. And this goes on and on, and all those sufferings which you have not lived are waiting for you. You have escaped...and you escape from one suffering to another, because a mind which was creating a suffering will create another. So you can escape from this suffering to that, but suffering will be there because your mind is the creative force.

Accept the suffering and pass through it; don't escape. This is a totally different dimension to work in. Suffering is there: encounter it, go through it. Fear will be there, accept it. You will tremble, so tremble. Why create a façade that you don't tremble, that you are not afraid?

If you are a coward, accept it.

Everyone is a coward. People you call brave are just façades. Deep down they are as cowardly as anyone else; rather, more cowardly. Just to hide that cowardliness they have created a bravery around them, and sometimes they act in such a way that everyone knows they are not cowards. Their bravery is just a screen.

How can man be brave?... Because death is there. How can man be brave?... Because man is just a leaf in the winds. How can the leaf help trembling? When the wind blows the leaf will tremble. But you never say to the leaf: "You are a coward." You only say that the leaf is alive.

So when you tremble and fear takes grip of you, you are a leaf in the wind. Beautiful – why create a problem out of it? But society has created problems out of everything.

If a child is afraid in the dark, we say: "Don't be afraid, be brave." Why? The child is innocent – naturally he feels fear in the dark. You force him: "Be brave." So he also forces, then he becomes tense. Then he endures the darkness but now tense; now his whole being is ready to tremble and he suppresses it. This suppressed trembling will follow him now his whole life. It was good to tremble in the darkness, nothing was wrong.

It was good to cry and run, nothing was wrong. The child would have come out of darkness more experienced, more knowing. And he would have realized, if he passed through darkness trembling and crying and weeping, that there was nothing to fear. Suppressed, you never experience the thing in its totality, you never gain anything out of it. Wisdom comes through suffering and wisdom comes through acceptance. Whatsoever the case, be at ease with it.

Don't look to society and its condemnation. Nobody is to judge you here and nobody can pretend to be a judge. Don't judge others and don't be perturbed and disturbed by others' judgment. You are alone and you are unique. You never were before, you never will be again. You are beautiful. Accept it. And whatsoever happens, allow it to happen and pass through it. Soon, suffering will be a learning; then it has become creative.

Fear will give you fearlessness. Out of anger will come compassion. Out of the understanding of hate, love will be born to you. But this happens not in a conflict, but in a passing-through with alert awareness. Accept, and pass through it. And if you make it a point to pass through every experience, then there will be death, the most intense experience. Life is nothing before it because life cannot be so intense as death.

Life is spread out over a long time – seventy years, one hundred years. Death is intense because it is not spread out – it is in a single moment. Life has to pass one hundred years or seventy years, it cannot be so intense. Death comes in a single moment; it comes whole, not fragmentary. It will be so intense you cannot know anything more intense. But if you are afraid, if before death comes you have escaped, you have become unconscious because of the fear, you have missed one of the golden opportunities, the golden gate.

If your whole life you have been accepting things, when death comes, patiently, passively you will accept and enter into it without any effort to escape. If you can enter death passively, silently, without any effort, death disappears. When Krishna, Christ, Buddha, Mahavira say you are deathless, they are not talking about a doctrine, they are talking about their own experience.

This can happen here in this camp also, because samadhi is death, dhyan is death, meditation is death. Many times there will be moments when you will suddenly feel you are dying. Don't escape, allow it to happen. If you allow it to happen, death has gone, death is there no more, and the inner flame, beginningless, endless, has come into being. It has always been there, now you can feel it.

So this should be the sutra. With fear, hate, jealousy, anything whatsoever, don't create a problem out of it. Accept it, allow it, pass through it, and you will defeat all suffering, all death. And you will become a jinna – a victorious one.

Anything more?

When you talk about our having to suffer, you tell us to be joyful at the same time. Trying to compromise these two things seems difficult.

When I say suffer joyfully it looks paradoxical and your mind starts thinking how to compromise both, because to you they are contradictory. They are not, they only appear contradictory. You can enjoy suffering.

What is the secret – how to enjoy suffering? The first thing is: if you don't escape, if you allow the suffering to be there, if you are ready to face it, if you are not trying somehow to forget it, then you are different. Suffering is there but just around you; it is not in the center, it is on the periphery. It is impossible for suffering to be in the center; it is not in the nature of things. It is always on the periphery and you are the center.

So when you allow it to happen, you don't escape, you don't run, you are not in a panic, suddenly you become aware that suffering is there on the periphery as if happening to someone else, not to you, and you are looking at it. A subtle joy spreads all over your being because you have realized one of the basic truths of life, that you are bliss and not suffering.

So when I say enjoy it I don't mean become a masochist; I don't mean create suffering for yourself and enjoy it. I don't mean: go on, fall down from a cliff, have fractures and then enjoy it, no. There are people of that type and many of them have become ascetics, tapasvis, and they are creating suffering for themselves.

They are masochists, they are ill. They are very dangerous people. They wanted to make others suffer but they were not so courageous. They wanted to kill others, be violent with others, cripple others, but they were not so courageous, so their whole violence has turned within. Now they are crippling themselves, torturing themselves, and enjoying it.

I am not saying be a masochist; I am simply saying suffering is there, you need not seek for it.

Enough suffering is there already, you need not go in search. Suffering is already there; life by its very nature creates suffering. Illness is there, death is there, the body is there\ by their very nature suffering is created. See it, look at it with a very dispassionate eye. Look at it\ what it is, what is happening. Don't escape. Immediately the mind says: "Escape from here, don't look at it." But if you escape then you cannot be blissful.

Next time you fall ill and the doctor suggests to remain in bed, take it as a blessing. Close your eyes and rest on the bed and just look at the illness. Watch it, what it is. Don't try to analyze it, don't go into theories, just watch it, what it is. The whole body tired, feverish\ watch it. Suddenly you will feel that you are surrounded by fever but there is a very cool point within you; the fever cannot touch it, cannot influence it. The whole body may be burning but that cool point cannot be touched.

I have heard about one Zen nun. She died, but before she died she asked her disciples: "What do you suggest? How should I die?"

It is an old tradition in Zen that masters ask. They can die consciously, so they can ask. And they are so playful even about death, so humorous about it, joking, laughing, they enjoy devising methods how to die.

So disciples may suggest: "Master, this will be good; die standing on your head." Or someone suggests: "Walking...because we have never seen anyone die walking."

So this Zen nun asked: "What do you suggest?"

They said: "It will be good if we prepare a fire, and you sit in it and die meditating."

She said: "This is beautiful and never heard of before." So they prepared a funeral pyre, the nun made herself comfortable in it, sat in a buddha posture, and then they lit the fire.

One man from the crowd asked: "How does it feel there? It is so hot that I cannot even come nearer to ask you\ that's why I am shouting. How does it feel there?"

The nun laughed and said: "Only a fool can ask such a question: How does it feel there? There it always feels cool, perfectly cool."

She is talking of her inner being, the center. There it is always cool, and only a foolish person can ask. Why does she say that only a foolish person can ask? It is obvious. When a person is ready to sit in the fire meditating, and then the fire is burnt and she is sitting silently, obviously it shows that this person must have achieved the innermost cool point which cannot be disturbed by any fire; otherwise, it is not possible.

So when you are lying on your bed feverish, on fire, the whole body burning, just watch it. Watching, you will recede towards the source. Watching, you will gain balance, a rhythm. Watching, not doing anything...what can you do? The fever is there, you have to pass through it; it is no use unnecessarily fighting with it. You are resting, and if you fight with the fever you will become more feverish, that's all. So watch it.

Watching fever, you become cool; watching more, you become cooler. Just watching, you reach to a peak, such a cool peak, even the Himalayas will feel jealous; even their peaks are not so cool. This is the Gourishankar, the Everest within. And when you feel that the fever has disappeared.... It has never really been there; it has only been in the body, very, very far away.

Infinite space exists between you and your body\infinite space, I say. An unbridgeable gap exists between you and your body. And all suffering exists on the periphery. Hindus say it is a dream because the distance is so vast, unbridgeable. It is just like a dream happening somewhere else\ not happening to you\in some other world, on some other planet.

When you watch suffering suddenly you are not the sufferer, and you start enjoying. Through suffering you become aware of the opposite pole, the blissful inner being. So when I say enjoy, I am saying: Watch. Return to the source, get centered. Then, suddenly, there is no agony; only ecstasy exists. Those who are on the periphery exist in agony. For them, no ecstasy. For those who have come to their center no agony exists. For them, only ecstasy.

When I say break the cup, it is breaking the periphery. And when I say be totally empty, it is coming back to the original source, because through emptiness we are born and into emptiness we return. Emptiness is the word, really, which is better to use than God, because with God we start feeling there is some person.

So Buddha never uses God, he always uses shunyata\emptiness, nothingness. In the center you are a non-being, nothingness, just a vast space, eternally cool, silent, blissful. So when I say enjoy I mean watch, and you will enjoy. When I say enjoy, I mean don't escape.

THE ROOT PROBLEM OF ALL PROBLEMS

The root problem of all problems is mind itself. The first thing to be understood is what this mind is, of what stuff it is made; whether it is an entity or just a process; whether it is substantial, or just dreamlike. And unless you know the nature of the mind, you will not be able to solve any problems of your life.

You may try hard, but if you try to solve single, individual problems, you are bound to be a failure – that is absolutely certain – because in fact no individual problem exists: mind is the problem. If you solve this problem or that, it won't help because the root remains untouched.

It is just like cutting branches of a tree, pruning the leaves, and not uprooting it. New leaves will come, new branches will sprout – even more than before; pruning helps a tree to become thicker. Unless you know how to uproot it, your fight is baseless, it is foolish. You will destroy yourself, not the tree.

In fighting you will waste your energy, time, life, and the tree will go on becoming more and more strong, far thicker and dense. And you will be surprised what is happening: you are doing so much hard work, trying to solve this problem and that, and they go on growing, increasing. Even if one problem is solved, suddenly ten problems take its place.

Don't try to solve individual, single problems – there are none: mind itself is the problem. But mind is hidden underground; that's why I call it the root, it is not apparent. Whenever you come across a problem the problem is above ground, you can see it – that's why you are deceived by it.

Always remember, the visible is never the root; the root always remains invisible, the root is always hidden. Never fight with the visible; otherwise you will fight with shadows. You may waste yourself, but there cannot be any transformation in your life, the same problems will crop up again and again and again. You can observe your own life and you will see what I mean. I am not talking about any theory about the mind, just the "facticity" of it. This is the fact: mind has to be solved.

People come to me and they ask: "How to attain a peaceful mind?" I say to them: "There exists nothing like that: a peaceful mind. Never heard of it."

Mind is never peaceful – no-mind is peace. Mind itself can never be peaceful, silent. The very nature of the mind is to be tense, to be in confusion. Mind can never be clear, it cannot have clarity, because mind is by nature confusion, cloudiness. Clarity is possible without mind, peace is possible without mind, silence is possible without mind – so never try to attain a silent mind. If you do, from the very beginning you are moving in an impossible dimension.

So the first thing is to understand the nature of the mind, only then can something be done.

If you watch, you will never come across any entity like mind. It is not a thing, it is just a process; it is not a thing, it is like a crowd. Individual thoughts exist, but they move so fast that you cannot see the gaps in between. The intervals cannot be seen because you are not very aware and alert, you need a deeper insight. When your eyes can look deep, you will suddenly see one thought, another thought, another thought – but no mind.

Thoughts together, millions of thoughts, give you the illusion as if mind exists. It is just like a crowd, millions of people standing in a crowd: is there anything like a crowd? Can you find the crowd other than the individuals standing there? But they are standing together, their togetherness gives you the feeling as if something like a crowd exists – only individuals exist.

This is the first insight into the mind. Watch, and you will find thoughts; you will never come across the mind. And if it becomes your own experience – not because I say it, not because Tilopa sings about it, no, that won't be of much help – if it becomes your experience, if it becomes a fact of your own knowing, then suddenly many things start changing. Because you have understood such a deep thing about mind, then many things can follow.

Watch the mind and see where it is, what it is. You will feel thoughts floating and there will be intervals. And if you watch long, you will see that intervals are more than the thoughts, because each thought has to be separate from another thought; in fact, each word has to be separate from another word. The deeper you go, you will find more and more gaps, bigger and bigger gaps. A thought floats and then comes a gap where no thought exists; then another thought comes, another gap follows.

If you are unconscious you cannot see the gaps; you jump from one thought to another, you never see the gap. If you become aware you will see more and more gaps.

**If you become perfectly aware,
then miles of gaps will be revealed to you.**

And in those gaps, satoris happen. In those gaps the truth knocks at your door. In those gaps, the guest comes. In those gaps God is realized, or whatsoever way you like to express it. And when awareness is absolute, then there is only a vast gap of nothingness.

It is just like clouds: clouds move. They can be so thick that you cannot see the sky hidden behind them. The vast blueness of the sky is lost, you are covered with clouds. Then you go on watching: one cloud moves and another has not come into the vision yet – and suddenly a peek into the blueness of the vast sky.

The same happens inside: you are the vast blueness of the sky, and thoughts are just like clouds hovering around you, filling you. But the gaps exist, the sky exists. To have a glimpse of the sky is satori, and to become the sky is samadhi. From satori to samadhi, the whole process is a deep insight into the mind, nothing else. Mind doesn't exist as an entity – the is the first thing. Only thoughts exist.

The second thing: the thoughts exist separate from you, they are not one with your nature, they come and go – you remain, you persist. You are like the sky: it never comes, it never goes, it is always there. Clouds come and go, they are momentary phenomena, they are not eternal. Even if you try to cling to a thought, you cannot retain it for long; it has to go, it has its own birth and death. Thoughts are not yours, they don't belong to you. They come as visitors, guests, but they are not the host.

Watch deeply, then you will become the host and thoughts will be the guests. And as guests they are beautiful, but if you forget completely that you are the host and they become the hosts, then you are in a mess. This is what hell is. You are the master of the house, the house belongs to you, and guests have become the masters. Receive them, take care of them, but don't get identified with them; otherwise, they will become the masters.

The mind becomes the problem because you have taken thoughts so deeply inside you that you have forgotten completely the distance; that they are visitors, they come and go. Always remember that which abides: that is your nature, your tao. Always be attentive to that which never comes and never goes, just like the sky. Change the gestalt: don't be focused on the visitors, remain rooted in the host; the visitors will come and go.

Of course, there are bad visitors and good visitors, but you need not be worried about them. A good host treats all the guests in the same way, without making any distinctions. A good host is just a good host: a bad thought comes and he treats the bad thought also in the same way as he treats a good thought. It is not his concern that the thought is good or bad.

Because once you make the distinction that this thought is good and that thought is bad, what are you doing? You are bringing the good thought nearer to yourself and pushing the bad thought further away. Sooner or later, with the good thought you will get identified; the good thought will become the host. And any thought when it becomes the host creates misery – because this is not the truth. The thought is a pretender and you get identified with it. Identification is the disease.

Gurdjieff used to say that only one thing is needed: not to be identified with that which comes and goes. The morning comes, the noon comes, the evening comes, and they go; the night comes and again the morning. You abide: not as you, because that too is a thought – as pure consciousness; not your name, because that too is a thought; not your form, because that too is a thought; not your body, because one day you will realize that too is a thought. Just pure consciousness, with no name, no form; just the purity, just the formlessness and namelessness, just the very phenomenon of being aware – only that abides.

If you get identified, you become the mind. If you get identified, you become the body. If you get identified, you become the name and the form – what Hindus call *nama, rupa,* name and form – then the host is lost. Then you forget the eternal and the momentary becomes significant. The momentary is the world; the eternal is divine.

**This is the second insight to be attained,
that you are the host and thoughts are guests.**

The third thing, if you go on watching, will be realized soon. The third thing is that thoughts are foreign, intruders, outsiders. No thought is yours. They always come from without, you are just a passage. A bird comes into the house from one door, and flies out from another: just like that a thought comes into you and goes out of you.

You go on thinking that thoughts are yours. Not only that, you fight for your thoughts, you say: "this is my thought, this is true." You discuss, you debate, you argue about it, you try to prove that: "this is my thought". No thought is yours, no thought is original – all thoughts are borrowed. And not second-hand, because millions of people have claimed those same thoughts before you. Thought is just as outside as a thing.

Somewhere, the great physicist, Eddington, has said that the deeper science goes into matter, the more it becomes a realization that things are thoughts. That may be so, I am not a physicist, but from the other end I would like to tell you that Eddington may be true that things look more and more like thoughts if you go deeper; if you go deeper into yourself, thoughts will look more and more like things.

In fact, these are two aspects of the same phenomenon: a thing is a thought, a thought is a thing.

When I say a thought is a thing, what do I mean? I mean that you can throw your thought just like a thing. You can hit somebody's head with a thought just like a thing. You can kill a person through a thought just as you can throw a dagger. You can give your thought as a gift, or as an infection. Thoughts are things, they are forces, but they don't belong to you. They come to you; they abide for a while in you and then they leave you. The whole universe is filled with thoughts and things. Things are just the physical part of thoughts, and thoughts are the mental part of things.

Because of this fact, many miracles happen – because thoughts are things. If a person continuously thinks about you and your welfare, it will happen – because he is throwing a continuous force at you. That's why blessings are useful, helpful. If you can be blessed by someone who has attained no-mind, the blessing is going to be true – because a man who never uses thought accumulates thought energy, so whatsoever he says is going to be true.

In all the eastern traditions, before a person starts learning no-mind, there are techniques and much emphasis that he should stop being negative, because if you once attain to no-mind and your trend remains negative, you can become a dangerous force. Before the no-mind is attained, one should become absolutely positive. That is the whole difference between white and black magic.

Black magic is nothing more than when a man has accumulated thought energy without throwing out his negativity beforehand. And white magic is nothing more than when a man has attained too much thought energy, and has based his total being on a positive attitude. The same energy with negativity becomes black; the same energy with positivity becomes white. A thought is a great force, it is a thing.

This will be the third insight. It has to be understood and watched within yourself.

Sometimes it happens that you see your thought functioning as a thing, but just because of too much conditioning of materialism you think this may be just a coincidence. You neglect the fact, you simply don't give any attention to it; you remain indifferent, you forget about it.

But many times you know that sometimes you were thinking about the death of a certain person – and he is dead. You think it is just a coincidence. Sometime you were thinking about a friend and a desire arose in you that it would be good if he comes – and he is on the door, knocking. You think it is a coincidence. It is not coincidence. In fact, there is nothing like coincidence, everything has its causality.

Your thoughts go on creating a world around you.

Your thoughts are things, so be careful about them. Handle them carefully! If you are not very conscious, you can create misery for yourself and for others – and you have done that. And remember, when you create misery for somebody, unconsciously, at the same time, you are creating misery for yourself – because a thought is a two-edged sword. It cuts you also simultaneously when it cuts somebody else.

One Israeli, Uri Geller, who has been working on thought energy, displayed his experiment on BBC television in England. He can bend anything just by thinking: somebody else keeps a spoon in his hand ten feet away from Uri Geller, and he just thinks about it – and the spoon bends immediately. You cannot bend it by your hand, and he bends it by his thought. But a very rare phenomenon happened on the BBC television; even Uri Geller was not aware that this is possible.

Thousands of people in their homes were seeing the experiment. And when he did his experiment, bent things, in many people's houses many things fell and became distorted – thousands of things all over England. The energy was as if broadcast. And he was doing the experiment at a ten-foot distance, then from the television screen in people's homes, around the area of ten feet, many things happened: things got bent, fell down, became distorted. It was weird!

Thoughts are things, and very very forceful things. There was one woman in Soviet Russia, Mikhailovana. She can do many things to things from far away, she can pull anything towards herself – just by thought. Soviet Russia was not a believer in occult things – a communist country, atheistic – so they had been working on Mikhailovana, on what is happening, in a scientific way. But when she does it, she loses almost two pounds of weight; in a half-hour experiment she loses two pounds. What does it mean?

It means that through thoughts you are throwing energy – and you are continuously doing it. Your mind is a chatterbox. You are broadcasting things unnecessarily. You are destroying people around you, you are destroying yourself.

You are a dangerous thing – and continuously broadcasting.

And many things are happening because of you. And it is a great network. The whole world goes on becoming every day more and more miserable because more and more people are on the earth and they are broadcasting more and more thoughts.

The further back you go, you find the earth the more and more peaceful – less and less broadcasters. In the days of Buddha, or in the days of Lao Tzu, the world was very very peaceful, natural; it was a heaven. Why? The population was very very small, for one thing. People were not thinkers too much, they were more and more prone to feeling rather than thinking. And people were praying. In the morning, they would do the first thing and that would be a prayer. In the night they would do the last thing – the prayer. And throughout the whole day also, whenever they would find a moment, they would be praying inside.

What is a prayer? Prayer is sending blessings to all. Prayer is sending your compassion to all. Prayer is creating an antidote of negative thoughts – it is a positivity.

This will be the third insight about thoughts, that they are things, forces, and you have to handle them very carefully.

Ordinarily, not aware, you go on thinking anything. It is difficult to find a person who has not committed many murders in thought; difficult to find a person who has not been doing all sorts of sins and crimes inside the mind – and then these things happen. And remember, you may not murder, but your continuous thinking of murdering somebody may create the situation in which the person is murdered. Somebody may take your thought, because there are weaker persons all around and thoughts flow like water: downwards. If you think something continuously, someone who is a weakling may take your thought and go and kill a person.

That's why those who have known the inner reality of man say that whatsoever happens on the earth, everybody is responsible. Everybody. Whatsoever happens in Vietnam, not only are the Nixons responsible, everybody who thinks is also responsible. Only one person can not be held responsible, and that is the person who has no mind; otherwise everybody is responsible for everything that goes on. If the earth is a hell, you are a creator, you participate.

Don't go on throwing responsibility on others – you are also responsible, it is a collective phenomenon. The disease may bubble up anywhere, the explosion may happen millions, thousands of miles away from you – that doesn't make any difference, because thought is a non-spatial phenomenon, it needs no space.

That's why it travels fastest. Even light cannot travel so fast, because even for light space is needed. Thought travels fastest. In fact it takes no time in travelling, space doesn't exist for it. You may be here, thinking of something, and it happens in America. How can you be held responsible? No court can punish you, but in the ultimate court of existence you will be punished – you are already punished. That's why you are so miserable.

People come to me and they say: "We never do anything wrong to anybody, and still we are so miserable." You may not be doing, you may be thinking – and thinking is more subtle than doing.

A person can protect himself from doing, but he cannot protect himself from thinking. For thinking everybody is vulnerable.

No-thinking is a must if you want to be completely freed from sin, freed from crime, freed from all that goes around you – and that is the meaning of a buddha.

A buddha is a person who lives without the mind; then he is not responsible. That's why in the east we say that he never accumulates karma; he never accumulates any entanglements for the future. He lives, he walks, he moves, he eats, he talks, he is doing many things, so he must accumulate karma, because karma means activity. But in the east it is said even if a buddha kills, he will not accumulate karma. Why? And you, even if you don't kill, you will accumulate karma. Why?

It is simple: whatsoever buddha is doing, he is doing without any mind in it. He is spontaneous, it is not activity. He is not thinking about it, it happens. He is not the doer. He moves like an emptiness. He has no mind for it, he was not thinking to do it. But if the existence allows it to happen, he allows it to happen. He has no more the ego to resist; no more the ego to do.

That is the meaning of being empty and a no-self: just being a non-being, anatta, no-selfness. Then you accumulate nothing; then you are not responsible for anything that goes on around you; then you transcend.

Each single thought is creating something for you and for others. Be alert!

But when I say be alert, I don't mean that think good thoughts, no, because whenever you think good thoughts, by the side you are also thinking of bad thoughts. How can good exist without bad? If you think of love, just by the side, behind it, is hidden hate. How can you think about love without thinking about hate? You may not think consciously, love may be in the conscious layer of the mind, but hate is hidden in the unconscious – they move together.

Whenever you think of compassion, you think of cruelty. Can you think of compassion without thinking of cruelty? Can you think of non-violence without thinking of violence? In the very word "non-violence," violence enters; it is there in the very concept. Can you think of brahmacharya, celibacy, without thinking of sex? It is impossible, because what will celibacy mean if there is no thought of sex? And if brahmacharya is based on the thought of sex, what type of brahmacharya is this?

No, there is a totally different quality of being which comes by not thinking: not good, not bad, simply a state of no-thinking. You simply watch, you simply remain conscious, but you don't think. And if some thought enters...it will enter, because thoughts are not yours; they are just floating in the air. All around there is a noosphere, a thoughtsphere, all around. Just as there is air, there is thought all around you, and it goes on entering on its own accord. It stops only when you become more and more aware. There is something in it: if you become more aware, a thought simply disappears, it melts, because awareness is a greater energy than thought.

Awareness is like fire to thought.

It is just like you burn a lamp in the house and the darkness cannot enter; you put the light off – from everywhere darkness has entered; without taking a single minute, a single moment, it is there. When the light burns in the house, the darkness cannot enter. Thoughts are like darkness: they enter only if there is no light within. Awareness is fire: you become more aware, less and less thoughts enter.

If you become really integrated in your awareness, thoughts don't enter you; you have become an impenetrable citadel, nothing can penetrate you. Not that you are closed, remember – you are absolutely open; but just the very energy of awareness becomes your citadel. And when no thoughts can enter you, they will come and they will bypass you. You will see them coming, and simply, by the time they reach near you they turn. Then you can move anywhere, then you go to the very hell – nothing can affect you. This is what we mean by enlightenment.

Sometimes you see in a madman's eyes an empty look – and madmen and sages are alike in certain things. A madman looks at your face, but you can see he is not looking at you. He just looks through you as if you are a glass thing, transparent; you are just in the way, he is not looking at you. And you are transparent for him: he looks beyond you, through you. He looks without looking at you; the "at" is not present, he simply looks.

Look in the sky without looking for something, because if you look for something a cloud is bound to come: "something" means a cloud, "nothing" means the vast expanse of the blue sky. Don't look for any object. If you look for an object, the very look creates the object: a cloud comes, and then you are looking at a cloud. Don't look at the clouds. Even if there are clouds, you don't look at them – simply look, let them float, they are there. Suddenly a moment comes when you are attuned to this look of not-looking – clouds disappear for you, only the vast sky remains. It is difficult because eyes are focused and your eyes are tuned to look at things.

Look at a small child the first day born. He has the same eyes as a sage – or like a madman: his eyes are loose and floating. He can bring both his eyes to meet at the center; he can allow them to float to the far corners – they are not yet fixed. His system is liquid, his nervous system is not yet a structure, everything is floating. So a child looks without looking at things; it is a mad look. Watch a child: the same look is needed from you, because again you have to attain a second childhood.

Watch a madman, because the madman has fallen out of the society. Society means the fixed world of roles, games. A madman is mad because he has no fixed role now, he has fallen out: he is the perfect drop-out. A sage is also a perfect drop-out in a different dimension. He is not mad; in fact he is the only sanest possibility. But the whole world is mad, fixed – that's why a sage also looks mad. Watch a madman: that is the look which is needed.

In old schools of Tibet they always had a madman, just for the seekers to watch his eyes.

A madman was very much valued. He was searched after because a monastery could not exist without a madman. He becomes an object to observe. The seekers will observe the madman, his eyes, and then they will try to look at the world like the madman. Those days were beautiful.

In the east, madmen have never suffered like they are suffering in the west. In the east they were valued, a madman was something special. The society took care of him, he was respected, because he has certain elements of the sage, certain elements of the child.

He is different from the so-called society, culture, civilization; he has fallen out of it. Of course, he has fallen down; a sage falls up, a madman falls down – that's the difference – but both have fallen out. And they have similarities. Watch a madman, and then try to let your eyes become unfocused.

In Harvard, they were doing one experiment a few years ago, and they were surprised, they couldn't believe it. They were trying to find out whether the world, as we see it, is so or not – because many things have surfaced within the few last years.

We see the world not as it is, we see it as we expect it to be seen, we project something onto it.

It happened that a great ship reached a small island in the pacific for the first time. The people of the island didn't see it, nobody! And the ship was so vast – but the people were attuned, their eyes were attuned to small boats. They had never known such a big ship, they had never seen such a thing. Simply their eyes would not catch the glimpse, their eyes simply refused.

In Harvard they tried it on a young man: they gave him spectacles with distorting glasses, and he had to wear them for seven days. For the first three days he was in a miserable state, because everything was distorted, the whole world around him was distorted.... It gave him such a severe headache, he couldn't sleep. Even with closed eyes those distorted figures would be there...the faces distorted, the trees distorted, the roads distorted. He couldn't even walk because he couldn't believe: "What is true and what is given by the projection of distorting glasses?" But a miracle happened! After the third day he became attuned to it; the distortion disappeared. The glasses remained the same, distorting, but he started looking at the world in the same old way. Within a week everything was okay: there was no headache, no problem, and the scientists were simply surprised; they couldn't believe it was happening. The eyes had completely dropped, as if the glasses were no longer there. The glasses were there, and they were distorting – but the eyes had come to see the world for which they were trained.

Nobody knows whether what you are seeing is there or not. It may not be there, it may be there in a totally different way. The colours you see, the forms you see, everything is projected by the eyes. And whenever you look fixedly, focused with your old patterns, you see things according to your own conditioning. That's why a madman has a liquid look, an absent look, looking and not looking together.

This look is beautiful. It is one of the greatest tantra techniques:

If one sees naught when staring into space...

Don't see, just look. For the beginning few days, again and again you will see something, just because of the old habit. We hear things because of old habit. We see things because of old habit. We understand things because of old habit.

One of the greatest disciples of Gurdjieff, P.D. Ouspensky, used to insist on a certain thing with his disciples – and everybody resented it, and many people left simply because of that insistence. If somebody said: "Yesterday you told..." he immediately would stop him and say: "don't say it like that. Say: 'I understood that you said this thing yesterday.' 'I understood....' don't say what I said; you cannot know that. Talk about what you heard." And he would insist so much because we are habitual.

Again you might say: "In the Bible it is said..." and he would say: "Don't say that! Simply say that you understand that this is said in the Bible." With each sentence he insisted: "Always remember that this is your understanding."

We go on forgetting. His disciples went on forgetting again and again, and every day, and he was stubborn about it. He would not allow you to go on. He would say: "go back. Say first that: 'I understand you said this, this is my understanding'...because you hear according to yourself, you see according to yourself – because you have a fixed pattern of seeing and hearing."

This has to be dropped. To know existence, all fixed attitudes have to be dropped. Your eyes should be just windows, not projectors. Your ears should be just doors, not projectors.

It happened: one psychoanalyst who was studying with Gurdjieff tried to do this experiment. In a wedding ceremony he tried a very simple but beautiful experiment. He stood by the side, people passing, and he watched them and he felt that nobody at the receiving end was hearing what they were saying – so many people, some rich man's wedding ceremony.

So he also joined in and he said very quietly to the first person in the receiving line: "My grandmother died today." The man said: "So good of you, so beautiful." Then to another he said it and the man said: "How nice of you." And to the groom, when he said this, he said: "Old man, it is time you also followed."

Nobody is listening to anybody. You hear whatsoever you expect. Expectation is your specs – that is the glasses. Your eyes should be windows – this is the technique.

Nothing should go out of the eyes, because if something goes a cloud is created. Then you see things which are not there, then a subtle hallucination.... Let pure clarity be in the eyes, in the ears; all your senses should be clear, perception pure – only then the existence can be revealed to you. And when you know existence, then you know that you are a Buddha, a god, because in existence everything is divine.

If one sees naught when staring into space;
if with the mind one then observes the mind...

First stare into the sky; lie down on the ground and just stare at the sky. Only one thing has to be tried: don't look at anything. In the beginning you will fall again and again, you will forget again and again. You will not be able to remember continuously. Don't be frustrated, it is natural because of so long a habit. Whenever you remember again, unfocus your eyes, make them loose, just look at the sky – not doing anything, just looking. Soon a time comes when you can see into the sky without trying to see anything there.

Then try it with your inner sky:

...If with the mind one then observes the mind...

Then close your eyes and look inside, not looking for anything, just the same absent look. Thoughts floating but you are not looking for them, or at them – you are simply looking. If they come it is good, if they don't come it is good also. Then you will be able to see the gaps: one thought passes, another comes – and the gap. And then, by and by, you will be able to see that the thought becomes transparent, even when the thought is passing you continue to see the gap, you continue to see the hidden sky behind the cloud.

And the more you get attuned to this vision, thoughts will drop by and by, they will come less and less, less and less. The gaps will become wider. For minutes together no thought coming, everything is so quiet and silent inside – you are for the first time together. Everything feels absolutely blissful, no disturbance. And if this look becomes natural to you – it becomes, it is one of the most natural things; one just has to unfocus, decondition:

...One destroys distinctions...
Then there is nothing good, nothing bad;
nothing ugly, nothing beautiful.
...And reaches buddhahood.

Buddhahood means the highest awakening. When there are no distinctions, all divisions are lost, unity is attained, only one remains. You cannot even call it "one," because that too is part of duality. One remains, but you cannot call it "one," because how can you call it "one" without deep down saying "two." No, you don't say that "one" remains, simply that "two" has disappeared, the many has disappeared. Now it is a vast oneness, there are no boundaries to anything.

One tree merging into another tree, earth merging into the trees, trees merging into the sky, the sky merging into the beyond...you merging in me, I merging in you...everything merging...distinctions lost, melting and merging like waves into other waves...a vast oneness vibrating, alive, without boundaries, without definitions, without distinctions...the sage merging into the sinner, the sinner merging into the sage...good becoming bad, bad becoming good...night turning into the day, the day turning into the night...life melting into death, death moulding again into life – then everything has become one.

Only at this moment is Buddhahood attained: when there is nothing good, nothing bad, no sin, no virtue, no darkness, no night – nothing, no distinctions. Distinctions are there because of your trained eyes. Distinction is a learned thing. Distinction is not there in existence. Distinction is projected by you. Distinction is given by you to the world – it is not there. It is your eyes' trick, your eyes playing a trick on you.

The clouds that wander through the sky have no roots, no home; nor do the distinctive thoughts floating through the mind. Once the self-mind is seen, discrimination stops.

The clouds that wander through the sky have no roots, no home... And the same is true for your thoughts, and the same is true for your inner sky. Your thoughts have no roots, they have no home; they wander just like clouds. So you need not fight them, you need not bc against them, you need not even try to stop thought.

This should become a deep understanding in you, because whenever a person becomes interested in meditation he starts trying to stop thinking. And if you try to stop thoughts they will never be stopped, because the very effort to stop is a thought, the very effort to meditate is a thought, the very effort to attain buddhahood is a thought. And how can you stop a thought by another thought? How can you stop mind by creating another mind? Then you will be clinging to the other. And this will go on and on, ad nauseam; then there is no end to it.

Don't fight – because who will fight? Who are you? Just a thought, so don't make yourself a battle ground of one thought fighting another. Rather, be a witness, you just watch thoughts floating. They stop, but not by your stopping. They stop by your becoming more aware, not by any effort on your part to stop them. No, they never stop, they resist. Try and you will find: try to stop a thought and the thought will persist. Thoughts are very stubborn, adamant; they are hath yogis, they persist. You throw them away and they will come back a million and one times. You will get tired, but they will not get tired.

And this is in fact the case. When you think you are tinged, it is just thinking. When you think that you have become good or bad, sinner or sage, it is just thinking, because your inner sky never becomes anything – it is a being, it never becomes anything. All becoming is just getting identified with some form and name, some colour, some form arising in the space – all becoming. You are a being, you are already that – no need to become anything.

Look at the sky: spring comes and the whole atmosphere is filled with birds singing, and then flowers and the fragrance. And then comes the fall, and then comes summer. Then comes the rain – and everything goes on changing, changing, changing. And it all happens in the sky, but nothing tinges it. It remains deeply distant; everywhere present, and distant; nearest to everything and farthest away.

A sannyasin is just like the sky: he lives in the world – hunger comes, and satiety; summer comes, and winter; good days, bad days; good moods, very elated, ecstatic, euphoric; bad moods, depressed, in the valley, dark, burdened – everything comes and goes and he remains a watcher. He simply looks, and he knows everything will go, many things will come and go. He is no more identified with anything.

Non-identification is *sannyas*, and *sannyas* is the greatest flowering, the greatest blooming that is possible.

In space shapes and colours form, but neither by black nor white is space tinged. From the self-mind all things emerge, the mind by virtues and by vices is not stained.

When Buddha attained to the ultimate, the utterly ultimate enlightenment, he was asked: "What have you attained?" He laughed and said: "Nothing – because whatsoever I have attained was already there inside me. It is not something new that I have achieved. It has always been there from eternity, it is my very nature. But I was not mindful about it, I was not aware of it. The treasure was always there, but I had forgotten about it."

You have forgotten, that's all – that is your ignorance. Between a Buddha and you there is no distinction as far as your nature is concerned, but only one distinction, and that distinction is that you don't remember who you are – and he remembers. You are the same, but he remembers and you don't remember. He is awake, you are fast asleep, but your nature is the same.

Try to live it out in this way – Tilopa is talking about techniques – live in the world as if you are the sky, make it your very style of being. Somebody is angry at you, insulting – watch. If anger arises in you, watch; be a watcher on the hills, go on looking and looking and looking. And just by looking, without looking at anything, without getting obsessed by anything, when your perception becomes clear, suddenly, in a moment, in fact no time happens, suddenly, without time, you are fully awake; you are a Buddha, you become the enlightened, the awakened one.

What does a Buddha gain out of it? He gains nothing. Rather, on the contrary, he loses many things: the misery, the pain, the anguish, the anxiety, the ambition, the jealousy, the hatred, the possessiveness, the violence – he loses all. As far as what he attains, nothing. He attains that which was already there, he remembers.

The Last Luxury

THE LAST LUXURY

In our civilization, professional people like me have a particular problem: we make too much use of our intelligence, so much so that we tend to view life through the intellect only, thus negating all other means of doing so. This tends to make life boring and dull, and robs it of its lustre.

No one can use his intellect too much. It is such a great force, with so much potential, that you cannot use it too much. Not only do you not use it too much, but you never even use it totally. Ordinarily, you do not use more than ten to fifteen percent of your total intellectual potential.

And another thing: when you do intellectual work it does not necessarily mean that you are using your intelligence. Intellectual work, too, is mechanical. Once you acquire the know-how, no intelligence is required at all; the mind works just like a computer.

The real problem is not the use of too much intelligence but the non-use of emotion. Emotion is completely disregarded in our civilization, so the balance is lost and a lopsided personality develops. If emotion is also used, then there is no imbalance.

A balance of emotion and intellect must be maintained in the proper ratio; otherwise the whole personality gets diseased. It is just like using only one leg. You may keep on using it, but you get nowhere; you simply tire yourself. The other leg must be used. Emotion and intellect are like two wings: when we use only one wing the outcome will be frustration. Then the bliss that comes from using both wings simultaneously, in balance and harmony, is never attained.

Don't be afraid of using the intellect too much. Only when intelligence is used do you touch the depths; only there is your potential stimulated. Intellectual work does not mean that your intelligence is being used.

Intellectual work is merely superficial; no depth is touched, nothing is challenged. That gives rise to boredom; it creates work that is without enjoyment. Enjoyment always comes when your individuality is challenged and you have to prove yourself and respond to the challenge. When challenged, intelligence or emotion both create their own bliss.

A person is schizophrenic if only one part of his personality is working and the other is dead. Then even the part that is working will not work really well because it will be overworked. Personality is a totality; it has no division at all. Actually, the whole personality is a flowing energy. When energy is used in a logical way it becomes intelligence, and when it is not used logically but emotionally it becomes the heart. These are two separate things; it is the same energy flowing through two different channels.

When there is no heart but only intellect, you can never relax.

Relaxation means that now the same energy within you is working in a different channel. Relaxation never means no-work, it means work in another dimension. Then the dimension that is overtaxed relaxes.

A person who follows an intellectual pursuit continuously, never relaxes. He does not divert his energy to another dimension, so his mind goes on working in only one direction unnecessarily. That creates boredom. Thoughts and more thoughts come and go; energy is diffused, wasted. You cannot enjoy it; on the contrary, you will be disappointed and disgusted with this unnecessary burden. But the mind, or the intellect, is not at fault. Because an alternative dimension has not been provided, because there is no other door open to it, the energy keeps circling round and round inside you.

Energy can never be stagnant. Energy means that which is not stagnant, that which is always flowing. Relaxation does not mean energy which is stagnant or asleep; scientifically, relaxation means that now energy is flowing through another channel, another dimension – it has entered another room.

But even though the room may be different, if it is not the very opposite of the room you were in before, the mind will not relax. For example, if you work on a scientific problem, then you can relax by reading a novel. The work is different: to deal with a scientific problem is to be active – a very masculine mode – whereas to read a novel is to be passive, which is an absolutely feminine mode.

Even though you are using the same mind you will be relaxed, because it is the opposite pole of the mind which is being used. You are not solving anything, you are not active; you are just a receiver, receiving something. The dimension is the same except that emotion, the opposite pole, is being brought into use.

In the same way, when we love, the intellect does not come into play at all. Quite the opposite happens: the irrational part of your personality comes into action. Intelligence must be balanced by love and love must be balanced by intelligence. Ordinarily, this balance is not found anywhere.

If someone is in love and begins to neglect all intellectual pursuits, this too will create boredom. Even love becomes a tension if it is a twenty-four-hour-a-day affair.

Once the challenge is lost, the enjoyment will also be lost: the play will be lost and it will become just work. The same thing happens with an intellectual who neglects the emotional side of his being.

These two parts, these two poles, must be in balance, only then is an integrated and individuated human being born; otherwise, whether emotional or intellectual, it will be the same disease. The east has become warped because it has been too concerned with the heart, while the west has been too concerned with the opposite pole. Both have achieved disastrous results.

In the west, the new generation is now rebelling against intellect, against reason. The whole mind of the new generation is leaning toward the irrational. Nature always takes its own revenge. Nature is very vengeful: it never pardons, it never forgets. If some part of it remains suppressed or unfulfilled it will have its revenge. In the west the irrational is taking its revenge. In the east the appeal is of the rational, the scientific: communism has much appeal and religion has lost its appeal. The irrational no longer appeals to the east because reason has been suppressed for too long.

To me, neither a human being nor a human culture can be healthy without an inner balance between the rational and the irrational. I do not take them to be two different things. I take them to be two poles of the same energy.

All energy can only exist between two opposite poles; energy requires an inner tension in order to create itself, in order to be. The poles can be negative and positive as in electricity, or north and south as in magnetism, or male and female as in biology, but energy cannot exist at only one pole. The opposite is needed in order to challenge, to stimulate, to create the necessary tension.

But in human society the other pole is always suppressed – either intellect is suppressed or emotion is suppressed.

A total culture has not come into existence yet, because there have only been civilizations of either the intellect or of the emotions. Culture, meaning a civilization in which the two poles function simultaneously, is as yet unborn.

Always balance one pole by its opposite. Then the more one pole is put to use, the more the opposite pole for which it is a relaxation will be illuminated. The mind must be capable of changing from one pole to the opposite pole just as easily as one moves from waking to sleeping. One must be able to be close to one dimension and remain open to the other. When this happens life is no longer dull; it becomes bliss.

Unfortunately, we become addicted to one polarity. Why is there this addiction to one extreme? We become addicted to one way of functioning because we have been trained for it. It is easier – you can function in the way that is familiar to you without any conscious effort – consciousness is not required.

When you change from one pole to the other, when you change your total perspective, you become an amateur. In this other realm you are not an expert; you are not trained in it. When you try to escape from it, then you tend to overburden that realm in which you are proficient.

This overdoing is the problem. One must not be an expert twenty-four hours a day; one must also do something in which one is a no one and about which one knows nothing. One must be a child sometimes: playing, immature, unknowing, ignorant.

Every genius has a child in him; no genius can exist without a child inside him – this child is the source of all his energy! Because of the child within him, sometimes he can be a novice, sometimes he can be totally ignorant: he can touch realms about which he knows nothing. A mathematician who turns to poetry is never a loser. He comes back to his mathematics with a purer mind, with new experiences that are unknown to mathematics.

Nothing has ever been invented or discovered by someone who is strictly professional. It is always discovered by one who approaches the subject like an outsider coming with the mind of a child. Only a child is inventive, never an old man. The old man is an expert, and an expert cannot invent.

He will go on repeating the same thing, doing it and overdoing it; he will make it more perfect but never new. A professional cannot contribute anything new to knowledge because he knows too much; he cannot see the new, he is always oblivious to the new. Professionals are always orthodox, they are never revolutionaries. They cannot be – their very being is heavy.

Whenever it happens that a scientist turns to poetry, or a poet turns to mathematics, or a businessman turns to painting, or a painter becomes a sannyasin, then something new is born.

And to give birth to something new is blissful; otherwise your daily work becomes dull and boring. Man cannot work like a machine – he cannot go on just producing the same things mechanically, repeating the same routine endlessly. If he goes on doing this, he will be completely dead long before he dies. He will only know that he has been alive when death comes.

If you are just functioning mechanically as a human machine, there is every danger that you will be replaced by a humanlike machine, and you can never be at ease, because whatever you can do can be done more efficiently by a mechanical device.

Society does not need individuality, it needs efficiency. So the more human a person becomes the less useful he is to society – and the more dangerous. The whole pattern of our civilization and, in fact, of all the civilizations that have existed in the world, is to turn the human being into an automaton. Then he is obedient, efficient and not dangerous. Otherwise a mind that is inventive, inquiring, seeking and searching for the new and always trying to give birth to something unknown, is bound to create disturbances. The establishment cannot be at ease with him.

Society begins to kill individuality as soon as a child is born.

Before he is seven, his individuality is killed completely. Only if by chance the establishment is not successful in doing this can a person become an individual. But this is rare. Every type of social institution is a means of killing the individual and converting him into a machine.

All our universities are factories to kill the spontaneous, to kill the spark, to kill the spirit and change man into a machine. Then the society feels at ease with him. He can be relied upon. The society knows what he can do, what he will do – he can be predicted. We can predict a husband, a wife, a doctor, a lawyer, a scientist. We know who they are and how they will react; we can be at ease with them. But it is impossible to be at ease with a person who is alive, spontaneous, because we don't know what he will do – he is unpredictable.

Unpredictability is always a source of insecurity. A wife cannot be at ease with a husband who is unpredictable. The moment he is unpredictable, he is unmanageable; he cannot be manipulated. No one is at ease with an unpredictable person – not even a father with an unpredictable son.

But only the unpredictable man can feel happiness, can feel like no one else. Life itself is unpredictable, unmanageable. Life as such always moves from moment to moment toward the unknown. It is an opening into the unknown – nothing more, nothing less.

If you are open, just like life itself, then you necessarily live in each of your dimensions: the physical, the intellectual, the emotional, the spiritual. Then you live totally; then there is no bifurcation, no division. Your energy flows as if from one room to another and then to another. There is no barrier to your energy; it is not pulled in any one direction, it is like a flowing river. Then you are always fresh and relaxed. Whenever you return to your particular field of work you approach it with a newness, a freshness that only comes from having relaxed in the opposite dimension.

The problem, as I see it, is not excessive intellectual work but too little or no work in the other dimensions, particularly the emotional. Reason is balanced by emotion. If you can do an exercise in logic but cannot weep, then you are bound to be in trouble. If you can only argue and not laugh, you are inviting trouble. But whenever a person appears whose life is like a flowing river it is difficult to understand him, because he cannot be categorized.

There is a Zen story:

A famous monk, who was a great teacher, died. He was best known, however, because of his chief disciple. Thousands of people came to pay homage to the monk when he died and to their amazement they found the chief disciple weeping. They were at a loss to understand him – an unattached person should not weep, especially one who has always said that the spirit never dies! Someone came and asked, "Why do you weep?"

The monk replied, "I cannot always live with 'whys.' There are moments when there is no why. I am weeping, that's all."

Still they insisted, "You have always said that the soul is immortal. Why do you weep then?"

He replied, "I still maintain that the soul is immortal. But that does not stop me from weeping."

This sounds illogical: if the soul is immortal, one should not weep. But the monk said, "The soul itself is weeping, and I cannot do anything about it. Whatsoever comes to me, I am one with it. Tears are coming, and I am one with them."

The monk's attitude cannot be categorized. We can understand someone's weeping if he believes that the soul is mortal. If he believes the soul to be immortal and does not weep, that too is understandable, it is all right. The soul is immortal: for whom to weep? No one has died. But the chief disciple had said that the soul is immortal and yet he was weeping. There was no why; the tears were just flowing.

The people asked, "Do you weep for the body?"

The monk said, "Yes, it must be for the body that I am weeping. The body, too, was beautiful and it will never be seen again. I weep for the body."

"But you are a spiritual man," they said. And the argument went on. They accused him of confusing them.

"I myself am confused," he said. "Life is such! The soul is important, but so are my tears. Such is life – so contradictory. It exists in contradictions. I myself am confused; but I am at ease with my confusions, I am at ease with my contradictions, so I am not tense. You see my tears, you see me weeping, but I am at ease. I am relaxed. I am blissful."

The other part must not be denied. The more you use reason, the more you must use the irrational to balance it. The moment it is balanced, you become weightless. You feel free. The weight of one is offset by the weight of the other; a balance is achieved. You are free.

Otherwise you will feel the burden, the weight, more and more until a moment comes when nothing exists but the burden. You are no more, only the burden will be felt; that is the only reality you will be conscious of. And the burden will be with you so continuously that you will not be able to conceive of what it is to be without it.

No one is without burden, but one burden can be balanced by another burden from the opposite pole. When the two burdens are balanced, there is no burden. A mind which is not burdened is not really a mind without burdens; rather, it is a mind with balanced burdens.

I am in favour of reason and no-reason existing together at the same time.

I advise a perpetual balance between the two. As soon as a burden is felt, know that the balance is lost and you must set about restoring it by adding the necessary weight wherever it is required. If the intellect is heavy, do something irrational. Meditate!

Meditation is not concerned with reason; it is irrational. So when someone asks me to explain meditation I am at a loss simply because there is no way that you can understand meditation. It is not concerned with logic, reason, arguments, and understanding at all. The only way to know it is to do it.

There are people who have been studying meditation all their lives and still have not understood it. They cannot. Krishnamurti talks about understanding it and makes understanding equivalent to meditation – as if meditation were something to be understood. Rather, understanding must be balanced by meditation, because meditation is the opposite pole, and once you try not to understand meditation you can do it.

If one goes on trying to understand meditation, there is less possibility of practicing it. There are people who say that they understand Krishnamurti perfectly. Intellectually, you can understand him, because understanding is intellectual. But even though he says intellectual understanding is not enough, still he equates understanding with meditation.

If intellectual understanding will not do, then only a nonintellectual jump will do.

In fact, there is no understanding that is not intellectual. Whenever you go into meditation it is less like understanding and more like feeling: it is felt, it is never understood.

Philosophy and science are intellectual processes; religion and art are non-intellectual processes. Philosophy must be balanced by religion and science must be balanced by art; otherwise a topsy-turvy, lopsided world is created in which everyone is diseased.

I have not come across a single individual who is at ease – something or other is always disturbing him. It does not matter what it is, all that matters is that he is disturbed. Everyone is disturbed! There must be something in our very concept of humanity which has gone wrong; something in the very structure of our society has gone wrong. People who are mentally disturbed are only symptomatic of what is happening to the whole society.

There is one very surprising fact: in the thirties, all the mental patients who visited psychoanalysts were primarily disturbed by violence. Then came the Second World War. The same thing had happened in the early twentieth century, and this was followed by the First World War. So as I see it, mental patients are the forerunners of us all: they herald that which is to come. In a way they are more sensitive; they perceive things before the rest of us do.

The same is true of artists. Everything that is to happen first happens in poetry, painting, music, etc.

If we look deeply into Picasso's art, for example, we will find the indication of a diseased civilization.

In his painting Guernica – or, for that matter, in any of his other works – he never portrays a human figure as it is. He never paints all the parts together or puts them in the right context. The head will be in one place, the neck somewhere else, and the eyes may be under the head. Such is his painting: schizophrenic, schizoid. He was an especially sensitive person who saw the shape of things to come, and the plight of the human being in times to come.

A society that is basically only scientific will be lacking in an aesthetic art – art will become ugly. All of western art has become ugly. Grotesqueness and absurdity have become the criteria. Ugliness is appreciated as greatness in art: the more ugly and distorted a painting, the more it is appreciated. There should be no harmony, no rhythm, no music; everything should be deranged and decayed like the present human mind.

These are indications and symptoms. They are symbolic expressions that the other side of the human mind is taking its revenge; it is demanding attention. A society which is basically only philosophic will be lacking in religion. And when a society becomes less and less religious, religion takes its revenge; it becomes ugly, ritualistic. A church and priesthood emerge and religion diminishes. The church is religion turned ugly, and the priest is the revenge of the prophet. The prophet has no place in the church, so the priest comes in and fills the vacuum.

We have not yet even conceived of a total culture, a total personality, a total mind. The totality is the sum total of the opposite polarities, so a totally consistent personality is an imperfect and partial personality which is, in a way, on the path to madness. This is dangerous. The part that has been denied expression and attention because of a consistent mind will take its revenge. The irrational will become aggressive; it will emerge with a vengeful force and will shatter all reason.

You must not only understand but also feel. It is not difficult to understand intellectually; the problem comes with feeling. You must also feel!

This can be possible only when you do something irrational. Jump and dance for an hour and you will see how relaxed and refreshed and alert you will feel. The mind becomes purified because the irrational is satisfied. Now reason can work freely without an enemy waiting to take revenge.

Give both sides of the mind an opportunity to express themselves freely; always balance the two. Live in these two complementary compartments:

the intellect and the emotions. They are not contradictory; they only appear so because we have been living at one extreme and have become fixated there.

When you dream you do not feel the contradiction and inconsistency of the dream – you see a friend approaching, and suddenly he turns into something else. But in the dream you take this as a fact; you feel no inconsistency, no contradiction. You do not ask how a man can change into an animal, because a dream has no logic; it still has to find its Aristotle.

In the dream you cannot say that if A is A then it cannot be B; if A is A it cannot be not A. In the dream, A can be not A and not A can be A. No logic is taken into account, nor is anything seen to be contradictory. So there are realms that are totally lacking in logic, but which are part of you all the same. Or it might be better to say that you are part of them, because the fact is that they are greater than you.

When contradictions are not seen to be contradictory, you are never bored. Are you ever bored in a dream? If a balance is achieved between the rational and the irrational, boredom vanishes. There is a moment-to-moment bliss. Every moment comes with a bliss of its own, otherwise life becomes a burden. But life is not responsible for this; we alone are responsible because the choice lies with us.

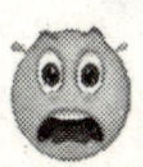